Hamilton Printing Company

Huntington directory

West Virginia 1891-2

Hamilton Printing Company

Huntington directory
West Virginia 1891-2

ISBN/EAN: 9783741183379

Manufactured in Europe, USA, Canada, Australia, Japa

Cover: Foto ©Andreas Hilbeck / pixelio.de

Manufactured and distributed by brebook publishing software
(www.brebook.com)

Hamilton Printing Company

Huntington directory

HUNTINGTON

(West Virginia)

DIRECTORY,

For 1891-2.

Embracing a Complete Alphabetical List of the
Residents of Huntington, W. Va.

—— together with a ——

Classified Business Directory,

CITY GUIDE, Etc.

compiled by

POTTS & CAMMACK,

General Real Estate and Insurance Agents,
Huntington, W. Va.

---

published by
HAMILTON PRINTING COMPANY,
DIRECTORY PUBLISHERS.
HAMILTON, OHIO

INDEX.

J. N. POTTS,

NOTARY PUBLIC

Has Notarial Seal.

324 NINTH STREET,

HUNTINGTON, W. VA.

ESTABLISHED 1844.

H. T. KENT,

JEWELER AND OPTICIAN,

WATCHES, CLOCKS, JEWELRY,

OPERA and FIELD GLASSES.

WE ISSUE NO CATALOGUES OR PRICE LISTS, BUT WILL SEND GOODS
FOR SELECTION TO RESPONSIBLE PARTIES.

58 W. Fifth St., Fountain Square,

CINCINNATI, O.

Huntington City Guide.

THE CITY OF HUNTINGTON.

The city of Huntington has fully 11,000 inhabitants. The Ensign Car Works are located here and employ in the neighborhood 1,100 men. The success of these works has been great, and is largely due to the advantages of a location that gives the company cheap fuel, cheap iron and cheap lumber.

The C. & O. R. R's principal shops are located here. employing at least 500 men. The leading religious denominations are represented here, and have good church buildings, and able and zealous men for pastors. Full directory for each church will be found in this book. The Hebrews have secured a splendid corner lot and will erect a magnificent temple on it. Huntington's Public Schools are of the very best, having four large buildings which cost about $70,000. In addition to the public schools, Marshall College, the largest normal school in the State. is centrally located here. It is the county seat of Cabell, and splendid public buildings will be erected on the south side of Fifth avenue between Seventh and Eighth streets. As a place for business or investment, Huntington has no superior in the State.

CITY OFFICERS.

Mayor—HAMILTON DICKEY.
Clerk—GEORGE H. MYERS.
Chief of Police—WILLIAM STALEY.
Treasurer—T. S. SCANLON.
Collector—F. D. BOYER.
Street Commissioner—J. S. STEWART.
Assessor—J. C. SWAIN.

COUNCILMEN.

FIRST WARD.
C. A. Boxley, J. L. McLellon, S. V. Mathews.

SECOND WARD.
Eli Ensign, D. B. Smith, H. B Vaughn.

THIRD WARD.
Charles Harrison, I. F. Stewart, Harry W. Jenkins.

SCHOOL COMMISSIONERS.
A. J. Beardsley, T. J. Bryan, B. H. Thackston, R. Enslow.
H. C. Simms.
Samuel Gideon, President.

CABELL COUNTY OFFICERS.

Clerk of Circuit Court.—B. C. Wilson, Term began January 1, 1891; expires December 31, 1896. (Democrat).

Clerk of County Court.—F. F. McCullongh, Term began January 1, 1891; expires December 31, 1896. (Democrat).

Prosecuting Attorney.—R. L. Blackwood. Elected to fill vacancy; term began 1890; expires December 31, 1892. (Democrat).

Surveyor of Lands.—J. L. Thornburg. Term began January 1, 1889; expires December 31, 1892. (Democrat).

Sheriff.—E. Kyle. Term began January 1, 1889; expires December 31, 1892. (Democrat).

County Commissioners.—T. A. Bias; term began January 1, 1889; expires December 31, 1894. (Democrat). B. H. Thackston; term began January 1, 1891; expires December 31, 1896. (Democrat). Geo. W. Grobe; term began January 1, 1887; expires December 31, 1892. (Democrat).

Assessor First District.—S. D. Hayslip. Term began January 1, 1889; expires December 31, 1892. (Democrat).

Assessor Second District.—Virgil Yates. Term began January 1, 1889; expires December 31, 1892. (Democrat).

STATE OFFICERS.

Governor.—Hon. A. B. Fleming, Marion County. Salary $2700 per annum. (Democrat).

Secretary of State.—Hon. Wm. A. Oxley, Marion County. Salary $1000 per annum and fees. (Democrat).

Superintendant of Free Schools.—B. S. Morgan, Monongalia County. Salary $1500. per annum. (Democrat).

Treasurer.—W. T. Thompson, Cabell County; salary $1400 per annum. (Democrat).

Auditor.—P. F. Duffy, Webster County. Salary $2000 per annum. (Democrat).

Attorney General.—Alfred Caldwell, Ohio County. Salary $1300 per annum. (Democrat).

Judges of Supreme Courts of Appeals.—Hon. D. B. Lucas, Jefferson County; salary $2200 per annum. (Democrat), Hon. J. W. English, Mason County; salary $2200 per annum. (Democrat), Hon. Henry Brannon, Lewis County; salary $2200 per annum. (Democrat). Hon. Homer A. Holt, Greenbrier County; salary $2200 per annum. (Democrat).

Adjutant General and Librarian.—B. H. Oxley, Lincoln County. Salary $1100 per annum. (Democrat).

SIXTH SENATORIAL DISTRICT.

Counties of Cabell, Wayne and Putnam. Hon. Jas. H. Marcum, (Democrat) of Cabell County, Senator. Term began January 7, 1891, and expires on the first Wednesday in January, 1895. Post office address, Huntington, W. Va.

Hon. B. J. Pritchard (Democrat), Wayne County, Senator. Post office address, Wayne C. H., W. Va.

BOOKS.   BOOKS.

LEVI CRIDER,

BOOKSELLER

AND

STATIONER,

Periodicals, Magazines and Daily Papers,

ALBUMS, BIBLES, GOLD PENS, ETC.,

School Books, Blank Books,

TABLETS, INKS AND SLATES.

VIOLINS, BANJOS, GUITARS AND HARMONICAS.

SPORTING GOODS, FISHING TACKLE,

HAMMOCKS, CROQUETS

And Base Ball Supplies.

LEVI CRIDER,

1011 Third Av., Huntington, W. Va.

FOURTH CONGRESSIONAL DISTRICT.

Counties of Pleasant, Wood, Richie, Wirt, Calhoun, Roane, Jackson, Mason, Wayne, Cabell, Putnam and Lincoln. Hon. James Copeheart (Democrat), of Mason County. Representative. Term began March 4, 1891, and expires March 4, 1893. Post office address, Point Pleasant, W. Va.

CIRCUIT COURT

Time of Holding Circuit Court in each County of the Eight Judicial Circuit.

HON. THOMAS H. HARVEY, JUDGE, Huntington, W. Va.

For the County of Cabell, the first Mondays in March, August and December.

For the County of Wayne, the first Mondays in February, June and September.

For the County of Lincoln, the third Mondays in February, June and September.

For the County of Logan, the first Mondays in April, July and October.

BOARD OF EDUCATION.

President, Samuel Gideon (R.); term expires 1892.
Secretary, James K. Oney (D.); elected yearly.
W. O. Wyatt (D.); term expires 1892.
R. Enslow (R.); term expires 1893.
H. M. Adams (R.); term expires 1891.
B. H. Thackston (D.); term expires 1891.

HUNTINGTON PUBLIC SCHOOLS.

The schools of Huntington, keeping pace with the growth of the city, have made marked progress, and now rank with the best in the state. The city's buildings are constantly inadequate.

The oldest building, comprising eight rooms, is located on Fourth avenue near Seventh street. Another of four rooms is on the corner of Third avenue and Twenty-second street. In 1888 was completed a ten room building at the junction of Fifth avenue and Thirteenth street, which is modern and first class in all its appointments, being fitted with the best of desks, heated and ventilated by the Smead system, and provided with the Smead dry closets.

Another building of eight rooms will be completed by September, 1891, at the corner of Sixth avenue and Twentieth street; and at the same time one of four rooms for the negro scholars will be built on Sixteenth street, both to be first class in every respect.

The teaching force now consists of a superintendent, teacher of vocal music and thirty-two teachers, and the enrollment of pupils, is 1612.

The course of study in our schools is fully up to the best, and is administered by an earnest and efficient corps of teachers.

The course includes nine years of eight months each, and a high

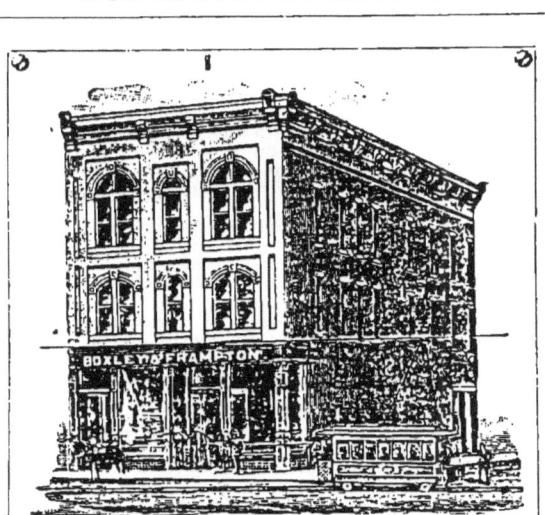

BOXLEY ⁘ & ⁘ FRAMPTON,

WHOLESALE AND RETAIL

GROCERS

Cor. 3d Ave. and 8th St.

HUNTINGTON: W. VA.

COUNTRY PRODUCE A SPECIALTY.

school course of three years, which will this year be lengthened to four years.

Aside from the regular branches of study, pupils are daily instructed in vocal music, drawing and physical culture. The high school course includes careful instruction in literature, current topics and elocution, with a special practical course of two years in book keeping. A special feature in the schools from the sixth grade upward is the daily instruction in composition under a special teacher, and excellent results are apparent.

A monthly magazine, "The School Mirror," is published by the superintendent, which is doing a good work in harmonizing patrons and teachers, giving to the people a clear understanding of the methods of the schools, and furnishing an incentive to pupils to do good composition work.

The system of examinations is such as to avoid stagnancy of intellect on the part of the teachers, in that instead of re-examining each year, those holding first grade certificates are examined on two or three additional studies each year, and credits for these added to their certificates.

Our citizens are justly as proud of their schools as of any other feature of our thriving young city.

BOARD OF TRADE.

J. K. Oney, President.   Frank A. Nash, Samuel Gideon. Vice-Presidents.   M C. Dimmock, Secretary.   W. H. H. Holswade, Treasurer.

The meetings of the Board of Trade will be held at the City Hall, on the first Tuesday night of each month, and members and citizens are urged to attend and participate in the meetings.

VOLUNTEER FIRE DEPARTMENT.

In all the different divisions of the department there are 95 able bodied firemen. The stations are located as follows:
Boone Engine House, No. 2, Central Station, 4th avenue, between 8th and 9th streets.
Victor Hose Co. corner 8th avenue and 10th street.
Canda Hose Co. 4th avenue and 23d street.
Ensign Hose Co. No. 4, corner 1st avenue and 24th street.
Hook and Ladder Co No. 1, at Central Station.
There are nine fire alarm signal boxes, located as follows:
Box No. 16, 3d avenue, West Huntington.
   "   12, corner 3d avenue and 9th street.
   "   34, corner 3d avenue and 12th street.
   "   271, corner 3d avenue and 19th street.
   "   62, corner 1st avenue and 23d street (Ensign office).
   "   44, Chesapeake & Ohio shops.
   "   25, corner 8th avenue and 20th street.
   "   53, corner 6th avenue and 10th street.
   "   5, Boone Engine House, Central Station.
Signal for "fire out" is two taps on the tower bell and on all the gongs. J. W. Boone, Chief Fire Department, and Superintendant Fire Alarm Telegraph. Jacob Elegar, Assistant Chief.

R. A. GOODWIN.   W. W. POINDEXTER.

CARROLLTON

✳ ✳ ✳ HOTEL. ✳ ✳ ✳

Opposite C. & O. Passenger Depot,

NINTH STREET,

HUNTINGTON, W. VA.

HUNTINGTON BELT LINE STREET RAILWAY.

C. L. Hafner, Sr., President; F. L. Doolittle, Secretary and Treasurer. Directors:—R. A. Goodwin, C. L. Hafner, Sr., F. L. Doolittle. F. F. McCullough, Rufus Switzer. Office and sheds, e s 10th st nr 7th av

BENEVOLENT SOCIETIES.

MASONIC.

Huntington Lodge, No. 53, F. & A. M. Meets in Masonic Hall, corner 10th street and 3d avenue, on the first and second Fridays of each month. John Olsen, W. M. Zenas Martin, Secretary.

Huntington Chapter, No. 22, R. A. M. Meets in Masonic Hall every second Friday. John Olsen, H. P. Zenis Martin, Secretary.

Huntington Commandery, No. 9, K. T. Meets in Masonic Hall every fourth Friday. M. C. Dimmick. E. C. Zenas Martin, Recorder.

Consistory No. 22, A. & A. Scottish Rite, 32° Meets in Masonic Hall upon the call of its officers. W. H. H. Holswade, 33° Ill. Com. in Chief. A. H. Woodworth, keeper of Seals and Records.

KNIGHTS OF HONOR.

Meets at Knights of Honor Hall, 3d avenue, between 9th and 10th streets, on the second and fourth Monday nights of each month. Thomas Sikes, Dictator. T. C. Palmer, Reporter. Rev. J. M. Sloan, Chaplain. J. L. Crider, Treasurer. A. H. Woodworth, Financial Reporter.

KNIGHTS AND LADIES OF HONOR.

Meets in K. of H. Hall on the first and third Monday nights of each month. H. C. Bossinger, Protector. Mrs. H. C. Bossinger, Vice-Protector. J. L. Crider, Secretary. A. H. Woodworth, Financial Secretary. Rev. J. M. Sloan, Chaplain. N. C. Petit, Treasurer.

BROTHERHOOD OF LOCOMOTIVE ENGINEERS.

Huntington Division, No. 190. Meets at old Masonic Hall, corner 3d avenue and 8th street, on the first and fourth Mondays, and second Friday of each month, at 1 P. M. A. S. Snedegar, C. E. T. J. Bullock, F. A. E. and I. N. S. A. F. Southworth, Jour. Agt.

G. A. R.

Baily Post, No. 4. Meets in I. O. O. F. Hall, corner 3d avenue and 10th street, on the fourth Tuesday of each month. George A. Floding, Commander. Mark Poore, Adjutant.

KNIGHTS OF PYTHIAS.

Meets in Palmer's Hall, 3d avenue between 8th and 9th streets, every Monday night. Dr. Carder, C. C. Geo. A. Floding, K. R. S.

THE

BAPTIST BANNER,

Published Weekly at $1.00 per Year,

——BY——

SADLER, MARTIN & Co.

⊛ITS JOB OFFICE⊛

Is in Good Shape for Turning Out All Kinds of
JOB WORK, from a

Business Card to a Large Pamphlet.

*SAMPLE COPIES OF THE
PAPER, AND ESTIMATES ON JOB WORK FREE
ON APPLICATION. Address,*

The Baptist Banner,

No. 930½ Fourth Avenue,

HUNTINGTON, W. VA.

I. O. O. F.

Huntington Lodge, No. 64. Meets in I. O. O. F. Hall, corner 3d avenue and 10th street, every Thursday night. Hiram C. Gordon, N. G. Frank D. Fuller, Secretary.

Cabell Encampment, No. 25. Meets in I. O. O. F. Hall on the first and third Tuesdays of each month. G. F. Klingel, C. P. C. N. Lallance, Scribe.

Canton Fidelity, No. 1, P. M. Meets at I. O. O. F. Hall on the second Friday of each month. Frank Hoff, Captain. B. F. Sites, Clerk.

I. O. R. M.

Mohawk Tribe, No. 11. Meets every Monday evening in Palmer's Hall. Jonas Carter, Sachem. A. W. Howard, C. of K.

GRAND UNITED ORDER OF ODD FELLOWS.

Meets first, second and third Mondays of each month, in their hall on 3d avenue, at 7:30 P. M. T. R. Jenkins, N. G. J. A. Manggrum, Secretary. W. O. James, D. L.

O. R. C.

Ashton Division, No 136, O. R. C. Officers for 1891: T. K. Hunsaker, C. C.; W. Waldron, S. and T. Meets in K of P Hall.

HOUSEHOLD OF RUTH.

Meets every fourth Monday of each month in hall of G. U. Odd Fellows. J. A. Manggrum, M. N. G. W. O. James, R. N. G. T. W. Wilkins, N. G.

CAMP GARNETT OF CONFEDERATE VETERANS.

"The object shall be to perpetuate the memory of fallen comrades and minister to the wants of those who were permanently disabled in the service; to preserve and maintain that sentiment of fraternity, born of the hardships and dangers shared in the march; the bivouac and the battlefield. We propose to avoid anything which partakes of partisanship in religion and politics, and at the same time we will lend our aid to the maintenance of law and the preservation of order."

The officers of this association consist of a Commander, to rank as Colonel; first, second and third Lieutenant-Commanders, to rank as Lieutenant-Colonels; Adjutant, Surgeon, Chaplain and Treasurer to rank as First Lieutenants.

J. N. Potts, Commander. B. A. Wolcott, Lieut-Commander. Jas. C. McClung, Lieut-Commander. James Dundas, Lieut-Commander. C. L. Thompson, Adjutant. Rev. J. M. Sloan, Chaplain. J. S. Sutphin, Treasurer. J. D. Myers, M. D., Surgeon.

CHURCHES.

FIFTH AVENUE BAPTIST CHURCH.

Pastors: Rev. W. P. Walker. D. D., and Rev. W. A. Nicholas. Clerk: J. N. Potts. Treasurer: Zenas Martin.

Deacons: J. N. Potts, J. H. Cammack, Zenas Martin, Robert Odell, H. M. Thornburg, F. D. Boyer, John Davies, Philip Rogers, Gordon Lunsford.

Finance Committee: J. N. Potts, Zenas Martin, A. F. Southworth, H. M. Thornburg, Robert Odell, F D. Boyer, John Davies, J. S. Marcum, David Heck, J. H. Cammack. Philip Rogers, Gordon Lunsford.

Secretary Mission Fund: R. R. Sadler. Financial Secretary, H. D. Stewart.

Meetings: Preaching every Lord's Day at 11 .00 a. m. and 7 :30 p.m. Sunday School at 9:45 a. m., J. N. Potts, superintendent.

Prayer Meeting. Every Wednesday at 7:30 p. m.

Communion Service. Second Lord's day in January, April, July and October.

Business Meeting. Wednesday preceding the second Lord's day in each month at 7:30 p. m.

Finance Committee. Meeting third Wednesday in each month after prayer meeting.

Financial Year closes December 31.

Benevolence: Collections for outside benevolent work will be taken as follows:

Education Board During February and March.

Foreign Missions, April and May.

State Missions, June and July.

Bible Board and Publishing Society, August and September.

A. Baptist Home Mission Society, October and November.

St. Cloud Mission S. S., 2 p. m., H. M. Thornburg, superintendent. Preaching 3 :00 p. m.

TWENTIETH STREET MISSION.

Preaching every Lord's day at 11 a.m. and 7:30 p. m. Sunday school at 9:45 a. m. J. H. Cammack, superintendent. Prayer meeting Thursday at 7:30 p. m.

FIRST PRESBYTERIAN CHURCH.

Fifth Avenue, between Tenth and Eleventh streets. Church Services: Sunday, preaching at 11 A. M., and at 7:30 P. M; Sunday School at 9:30 A. M. Wednesday, prayer meeting at 7:30 P. M. Friday, Young People's Meeting at 7:30 P. M. Jos. M Sloan, Pastor. J. L. Johnston, Job Webb, H. M. Adams. J C. Dickey, Elders. W. H. H. Holswade, Jas. S. Miller, Jas. M. Lee, A. C. Thomas, Deacons.

FIRST CONGREGATIONAL CHURCH.

South-east corner Fifth Avenue and Ninth street. Preaching at 11 o'clock A. M. and 7:30 P. M. Sunday School meets at 9:45 A. M. Prayer meeting Wednesday night.

Rev. J. L. Collier Pastor, Benjamin P. Driggs, E. J. Davis, H. S. Osgood, A. T. Higgins. Deacons. H. M. Ensign, Clerk. A. T. Higgins, Treasurer. D. E Abbott, R. S Carr, W. J. Parsons, Trustees. R. S. Carr, Superintendent Sunday School. A. T. Higgins, Assistant

Superintendent Sunday School. B. L. Davis, Secretary. Miss Clara Spangenburg, Treasurer. Mrs. A. M. Poore, President Ladies Circle. Mrs. H. Spangenburg, Secretary Ladies Circle. Mrs. H. S. Osgood, Treasurer Ladies Circle.

FIRST M. E. CHURCH.

Corner Fourth avenue and Tenth street. Rev. W. Wirt King, pastor.
Regular services Sunday at 11 and 7:30
Sunday School. M. N. Hambleton, superintendent. at 9:30 a. m.
Prayer and praise service, Wednesday evening at 7:30.
Class meeting Sunday at 12 o'clock.
Young People's meeting, Friday evening at 7:30
Epworth League meeting, Sunday at 3 p. m.
Trustees:—R. Shore, J. L. Crider, T. C. Palmer, H. C. Bossinger, K. Delebar, J. L. Woods.
Stewards:—A. B. Palmer, T. C. Palmer, J. L. Crider, H. C. Bossinger, K. Delebar, H. Gordon, G. W. R. Snyder, R. Turney, A. J. Bagby, George A. Floding, J. T. Woods, M. N. Hambleton.

METHODIST EPISCOPAL CHURCH, SOUTH.

Fourth avenue, between Tenth and Eleventh streets. Rev. J. A. Black, Pastor. H. A. Ware, Sunday School Superintendent. Thos. Medford, Assistant Sunday School Superintendant. Richard Woods, Class Leader. Board of Stewards: H. C. Harvey, Chairman. T. W. Peyton, Secretary. L. H. Borks, Treasurer. C. H. Ricketts. J. E. Blanchard, L. E. Black. L. S. McGlathery. Services: Sunday School 9:30 a. m. Preaching, 11 a. m. and 7:30 p. m. Prayer meeting Wednesday 7:30 p. m. Class meeting Thursday 7:30 p. m. Societies: Epworth League meets every Monday at 7:30 p. m. Woman's Missionary Society meets the third Saturday in each month at 3 p. m. Juvenile Missionary Society meets the third Sunday in each month at 3 p. m. The Ladie's Aid Society meets Thursday of each week at 3 p. m.

CATHOLIC CHURCH.

Church of St. Joseph. Rev. J. W. Werninger, Pastor, corner Sixth avenue and Thirteenth street.

HEBREW CONGREGATION.

Rev. S. K. Lewis. Services every Friday evening at 7:30. Sunday School every Saturday at 10 a. m. and Sundays at 10 a. m. Present place of meeting at Knights of Honor Hall. Temple now in progress at Tenth street and Fifth avenue. Officers: S. Gideon, Pr. L. Shyer, Vice Pr. Lee Kahn, Secretary. L. Sternberger, Treasurer. Trustees: M. Broh, L. Keiner. Jacob Zigler. The above congregation has also beautiful lots in Spring Hill Cemetery.

MT. OLIVE BAPTIST CHURCH (COLORED).

North side Eighth Avenue, between Eighth and Ninth streets. Rev. I. V. Bryant, Pastor. G. W. Winston, Clerk. R. A. Woodson, Treasurer. Wm. O. James, James Manggrum, and John Michens, Trustees. J. M. Jasper, Alex. Winston, Winston Boyd. R. A. Woodson, John Michens, and Thomas Wilkins, Deacons. Services: Preaching every

Sunday at 11 o'clock a. m. and 7 o'clock p. m.   Prayer meeting Monday
and Wednesday at 7 o'clock p. m.   Sunday School at 9:30 a. m.   Wm.
Johnson, Superintendent.   Special Meetings: Regular business meetings on Thursday preceding the third Sunday in each month. Communion third Sunday in each month at 3 o'clock p. m.

EBENEZER M. E. CHURCH.

Eighth avenue and 16th street. Rev. Daniel Aguilla, pastor.
Wm. Morgan, John Allen, Robert Humphrey, Trustees.
John Allen, John Griffin, Richard Anderson, Stewards.
John Griffin, Superintendent Sunday School.
Preaching every Sunday at 11 a. m. and 7:30 p. m.   Prayer meet-
ing every Wednesday at 7:30 p. m.

STREET DIRECTORY.

All streets run north to south.   Avenues run from east
to west.

First street runs to Seventh avenue
Second street runs to Twelfth avenue
Third street runs to Twelfth avenue
Fourth street runs to Thirteenth avenue
Fifth street runs to Thirteenth avenue
Sixth street runs to Thirteenth avenue
Seventh street runs to Thirteenth avenue
Eighth street runs to Thirteenth avenue
Ninth street runs to Thirteenth avenue
Tenth street runs to Thirteenth avenue
Eleventh street runs to Thirteenth avenue
Twelfth street runs to Eighth avenue
Thirteenth street runs to Eighth avenue
Fourteenth street runs to Eighth avenue
Fifteenth street runs to Eighth avenue
Sixteenth street runs to Eighth avenue
Seventeenth street runs from Third avenue to Fifth avenue, then
from Eighth avenue to Tenth avenue
Eighteenth street runs from Third avenue to Fifth avenue, then
from Eighth avenue to Twelfth avenue
Nineteenth street runs from Third avenue to Seventh avenue, then
from Eighth avenue to Twelfth avenue
Twentieth street runs from First avenue to Twelfth avenue
Twenty-first street runs from First avenue to Twelfth avenue
Twenty-second street runs from First avenue to Twelfth avenue
Twenty-third street runs from First avenue to Eleventh avenue
Twenty-fourth street runs from river bank to Tenth avenue
Twenty-fifth street runs from river bank to Sixth avenue
Twenty-sixth street runs from river bank to Sixth avenue
Twenty-seventh street runs from river bank to Sixth avenue
Twenty-eighth street runs from river bank to Seventh avenue
Twenty-ninth street runs from Third avenue to Seventh avenue
Thirtieth street runs from Third avenue to Seventh avenue
Thirty-first street runs from Third avenue to Seventh avenue
First avenue commences Twentieth street, running east to Thirty-
first street

Second avenue commences First street, running east to Sixteenth street, then from Twenty-fifth to Thirty-eighth street

Third avenue commences First street, running east to Thirty-first street

Fourth avenue commences First street, running east to Sixteenth street, then from Seventeenth to Thirty-first streets

Fifth avenue commences First street, runs to Sixteenth street, then from Eighteenth to Thirty-first streets

Sixth avenue commences First street, runs to Sixteenth street, then from Twentieth to Twenty-fourth streets and from Seventeenth to Thirty-first streets

Seventh avenue commences First street, runs to Sixteenth street, then from Nineteenth to Thirty-first streets

Eighth avenue commences Second street, runs to Twenty-fourth street

Ninth avenue commences Second street, runs to Eleventh street, then from Seventeenth to Twenty-fourth streets

Tenth avenue commences Second street, runs to Eleventh street, then from Eighteenth to Twenty-fourth streets

Eleventh avenue commences Second street, runs to Twelfth street, then from Eighteenth to Twenty-second streets

Twelfth avenue commences Second street, runs to Twelfth street, then from Eighteenth to Twenty-second streets

Thirteenth avenue commences Fourth street, runs to Twelfth street

Virginia avenue commences at Seventeenth street, runs to Twentieth street, between Third and Fourth avenues

College avenue commences at Seventeenth street, runs to Twentieth street, between Fourth and Fifth avenues

Maplewood avenue commences at Nineteenth street, runs to Twentieth street, between Fifth and Sixth avenues

Buffington avenue commences at Nineteenth street, runs to Twentieth street, between Sixth and Seventh avenues

Locust avenue commences at Nineteenth street, runs to Twentieth streeth, between Seventh avenue and Railroad

Artisan avenue commences at Seventeenth street, runs to Twentieth street, between Eighth and Ninth avenues

Odd numbers are on the right and even numbers on the left going east on the avenues, or south on the streets

On crossing a street or avenue, the numbers begin with even hundreds. Thus: starting at Eighth street on Third avenue, the first number is 801; the last number in that square will be 856; but begins again on east side of Ninth street, 901. The same rule holds in going south on the streets. The first number south of Second avenue is 201, and so on of all the avenues

POTTS & CAMMACK'S

HUNTINGTON CITY DIRECTORY,

FOR 1891-2

ABBREVIATIONS.

av	Avenue	n e	north east
b	between	nr	near
bds	boards	opp	opposite
cor	corner	R. R.	railroad
confec	confectioner	res	residence
corp	corporation	s	south or side
e	east	s e	south east
manuf	manufacturer	w	west
n	north	wks	works

A

Abbott D. E. proprietor Eureka Copying House. 910 4th av, res 6th av b 9th and 10th

Abbott Mrs. A. M. 1138 6th av

Abshire Emma, s s 3d av, West Huntington

Abshire Fannie, s s 3d av, West Huntington

Abshire William, teamster, s s 3d av, West Huntington

Adams A. J. wks Ensign Co. res 1911 6th av

Adams Al. shipping clerk C. & O. 909 2d av

Adams D. P. & Co. (D. P. A. & C. F. Cole) plumbers and gas fitters, 1115 3d av

Adams D. P. (D. P. A. & Co.) res 1111 4th av

Adams E. W. dairyman, 1037 3d av, res same

Adams E. W. laborer, res 16 Frame Row

Adams Eliza, dressmaker, 16 Frame Row

Adams Mrs. Emma, 733 6th av

ADAMS EXPRESS COMPANY, general forwarders of freight, 1038 3d av, J. M. Wyatt, agent

Adams Frank, clerk 833 3d av. bds 733

Adams H. M. (Postmaster) grocer, 1010 3d av, res 1043 4th av

Adams J. A. mail agent, bds 641 5th av

Adams J. Q. grocer 833 3d av, res 733 6th av

Adams & Price, grocers, 1010 3d av

Adams Rosie B. 16 Frame Row

Adams T. W. machinist, res 1913 6th av

Adams W. E. watchman, res 1929 Buffington av

Adams W. H. dairyman 807 9th av, res same

Adams William, machinist, 1936 Maple av

Adams Will W. engineer water works, res 1111 4th av

Adkins Alex, drayman, alley b 3d and 4th avs and 11th and 12th sts

Adkins Belle, dressmaker, 703 3d av

Adkins B. S. clerk, bds 703 3d av

Adkins Bert, merchant, 707 3d av, res 701 3d av

Adkins Delilah, 317 11th st alley

Adkins Dollie, 703 3d av

Adkins Edna, school teacher, 703 3d av

Adkins Elisha, grocery and restaurant, 814 3d av

Adkins Ella, res Buffington Row

Adkins Mrs. Emma, 740 3d av

Adkins Enoch, clerk, bds 902 7th av

Adkins Francis, 222 8th st

Adkins Harvey, m'gr Continental Hotel, 801 2d av

Adkins James O. 317 11th st alley.

Adkins James, drayman, 222 8th st

Adkins John, 317 11th st alley

Adkins John, teamster, 222 8th st

Adkins L. L. restaurant 814 3d av

Adkins Lee, wks Ensign Co., bds 829 3d av

Adkins Leige, butcher, 1055 3d av, res s s 3d av b 19th and 20th

Adkins Mrs. Mary, restaurant, 814 3d av

Adkins Mattie, clerk, 701 3d av

Adkins Nancy, school teacher, 703 3d av

Adkins Nancy E. 222 8th

Adkins Nathaniel, blacksmith, alley b 3d and 4th avs and 11th and 12th sts

Adkins Nevada, 703 3d av

Adkins Noah, merchant, 701 3d av, res same

Adkins P. G. grocer, 1021 6th av, res same

Adkins Riley, grocer, 701 2d av, res 701 alley

Adkins Sherman, hod carrier. 1221 3d av alley

Adkins Tolbert (A. Bros.), merchant, 816 3d av, res 740 3d av

Adkins W. H. bar keeper, e s 8th b 2d and 3d av

Adkins Wm. yard foreman, res s of 4 pole

Adkins Wm. teamster, alley b 3d and 4th avs and 10th and 11th

Adkins Wm. farmer, res Buffington Row

ADVERTISER PUBLISHING CO. W. H. Banks, President, publishers Daily and Weekly Advertiser, 845 3d av

Agnew Albert, car maker, res 710 3d av

Agnew Mrs. J. W. boarding house, 1007 3d av

Ahern Daniel, machinist, 1343 3d av

Ailstock Ed. machinist, bds 2335 8th av

Ailstock V. res 2335 8th av

Alderman Anderson, res 18 Frame Row

Alderman Daniel W. carpenter, 18 Frame Row

Alderman Henry, carpenter, 18 Frame Row

Alderman Isaac W. 18 Frame Row

Aldine Roller Mills, Gwinn Bros. propr, 954 2d av

Allen Seward, fireman, 1011 6th av

Allensworth W. H. brakeman, 711 6th av

Alley E. W. machinist, bds 313 11th

Alley Peyton, laborer, bds 313 11th

Anchor Bottling Works, B. B. Harding, prop, 947 2d av

Anderson Charles, cook Continental Hotel

Anderson George, 1131 4th av

Anderson James, cook Continental Hotel

Anderson L. cook Continental Hotel

Anderson Lena, res 1678 8th av

Anderson Pendleton, wks C & O shops, bds 1660 8th av

Anderson S. L. call boy, 629 w 9th st

Anderson Samuel, drayman, 419 11th st

Anderson Wm. laborer, res 1678 8th av

Anderson Wm. laborer, res 1925 3d av

Andre Charles A. railroad fireman. 1690 9th av

Andrews J. A. wks C & O, bds 3 Brick Row

Andrews R. A. real estate agent 924 3d av, res 1135 6th av

Angel Maggie, compositor, bds 4th av and 17th

Aquila Rev. Daniel, pastor Colored Methodist Church, 808 16th st

Archer Frank M. student. 516 9th st

Archer R. M. salesman, 516 9th st

Archer Robert L. bank clerk, 516 9th st
ARGUS PRINTING HOUSE, W. F. and G. E.
　　Wallace, proprietors, publishers Weekly Argus, 934
　　4th av
Armstrong C. E. teamster, 1917 8th av
Armstrong T. N. engineer, bds 828 6th av
Armstrong W. H. druggist, 934 3d av, res 529 12th st
Armstrong Wilbert, laborer, 1917 8th av
Arnett Frank, brakeman, bds 1011 6th av
Arnett William, lumber inspector, bds 1011 6th av
Arthur Effie, 11 Buffington Row
Arthur John L. blacksmith, 1901 Buffington av
Arthur L. C. blacksmith, res 1715 4th av
Arthur William, painter, 11 Buffington Row
Arthur Mrs. Wm. 2213 3d av
Asbury A. C. carpenter, 1827 3d av
Asbury Anna 1827 3d av
Asbury H. W. coal dealer, 1827 3d av
Asbury I. A. butcher, 1827 3d av
Ashworth L. J. merchant, 1831 3d av, res same

B

Baer Peter, Five Cent Store, 1041 3d av
Baer Mrs. P. saleslady, 1041 3d av
Bagby A. W. carpenter, 739 4th av
Bagby Mrs. Maud L. dressmaker, 739 4th av
Bagley Martin, laborer, res 10 n Ensign shops
Baily Emma, cook, 1111 6th av
Baily J. W. clerk, 309 10th st
Baily Wiley, hod carrier, 812 7th av alley
Baker Mrs. Adeline, 739 alley b 4th and 5th avs and 7th
　　and 8th sts
Baker Andrew, brakeman, rms 731 3d av
Baker Miss C. A. 1120 7th av
Baker C. C. brakeman, bds 828 6th av
Baker R. H. grocer, res 1921 3d av
Baker Stephen, laborer, 1212 4th av alley
Baldwin Howard, painter, 1926 Locust av
Baldwin S. M. blacksmith, res 1926 Locust av
Ballard J. H. laborer, 1130 3d av
Ballard Patterson, freight handler, 1042 3d av alley

Balsley W. T. auctioneer, 743 alley b 4th and 5th avs and 7th and 8th sts

Banks John, porter St. Nicholas Hotel

BANKS W. H. President Advertiser Publishing Co. and chief clerk Ensign Co. res 1117 5th av

Banks William, brakeman, bds 731 3d av

BAPTIST BANNER (The), Sadler, Martin & Co. publishers, 930½ 4th av

Barber W. S. artist, bds 1328 4th av

Barkly, Clarence, student, 1030 6th av

Barkly Edgar J. machinist, 1030 6th av

Barkly William, machinist, 1030 6th av

Barnett B. L. laborer, res 35 Buffington Row

Barnett J. C. foreman Ensign Co. res 2145 3d av

Barnett John T. 35 Buffington Row

Barnett Lelila, 35 Buffington Row

Barnett Reuben, fireman, res 1854 8th av

Barnett W. F. machinist, 315 12th st

Barnes Mrs. A. E. dress maker, 1316 4th av

Barnes C. L. brick mason, 1316 4th av

Barnes John S. bds cor 16th st and 20th av

Barnes Wm. L carpenter, res 2311 8th av

Barr Mrs. M. A. res 2335 8th av

Barrett John H. railroad employe, bds 1660 8th av

Barringer Asa, carpenter, res 15 Frame Row

Barrows Millard, engineer, res 2137 3d av

Bates Edward, machinist, bds 1832 4th av

Bates John W. watchman, res n 24th st

Bates Samuel, n 24 st

Baumgardner Anna, 1222 3d av

Baumgardner Harry, grocery clerk, 521 w 9th st

Baumgardner James M. crossing watchman, 521 w 9th st

Baumgardner Mrs. Rebecca, dress maker. 525 w 9th st

Baxter & Co. stoves and tinware, 753-5 3d av

Baxter Coleman, tinner, cor 3d av and 8th st, res 739 2d av

Baxter George, tailor, 854 3d av, bds 1245 3d av

Baxter R. tinner, res 739 2d av

Beach S. C. 1016 4th av

Beal Maggie, domestic, 1037 4th av

Beal Peter, barber, 937 3d av, res 1015½ 3d av

Beales E. D. shoe maker, 223 9th st, res 1105 4th av

Beales George A. painter, res 1105 4th av

Beard Mrs. Minerva, 1819 8th av

Beardsley A. J. physician and surgeon, 1003 3d av, res 1125 3d av
Beardsley Mrs. A. J. 1125 3d av
Beardsley Lola, teacher, 1125 3d av
Beardsley Willie, 1125 3d av
Beatty Mrs. Addie, 537 w 9th st
Beckett C. W. moulder, res 1947 6th av
Beckett F. M. carpenter, res 1915 5th av
Beckwith Wesley, plasterer, n s alley b 2d and 3d avs and 7th and 8th sts
Behrend H. bartender, 1009 3d av, res 4th av b 10th and 11th sts
Bell Amanda, 739 8th st
Bell Edgar, carpenter, 1205 3d av
Bell Peter, laborer, 739 8th st
Bell Thomas, machinist, bds.926 6th av
Bellamy Georgia, seamstress, res 920 6th av alley
Bellamy Henry, policeman C. & O. shops, res 920 6th av alley
Bender Charles, carpenter, res 2144 4th av
Bennett Hon. E. A. real estate agent, cor 16th st and 19th av, res cor 16th st and 20th av
Bennett Edward, cor 16th st and 20th av
Bennett John, car builder, res 1730 4th av
Bennett John, telegraph opr, cor 16th st and 20th av
Benshoff W A. bill clerk, res 918 4th av
Berge Alice, domestic, 916 5th av
Berry J. insurance, res 1123½ 3d av
Berry James, saddler, res 913 5th av
Berry John M. grocer, 1001 6th av, res 10th st b 5th and 6th avs
Berry Mrs. Mary A. groceries and bakery, 1123½ 3d av
Berry Samuel, fireman, res 2 n Ensign
Berry W. clerk, res 10th st b 5th and 6th avs
Bess Mrs. H. A. 2003 3d av
Bess I. A. teamster, 5 Buffington Row
Bess Mary A. 5 Buffington Row
Best J. A. drayman, 733 alley b 7th and 8th sts and 4th and 5th avs
Beswick Samuel, contractor, res 1406 4th av
Beuhring Mrs. E. O. 1236 4th av
Bevan Alfred S. car builder, res 1728 4th av
Bevan M. M. car builder, 1711 Virginia av
Bevan Sadie, compositor, bds Virginia av b 3d and 4th avs

Bias Geo. W. laborer, res 420 17th st
Bibber Wade, 1031 4th av
Bick Arthur, 1832 5th av
Bick Chas. blacksmith, res 1832 5th av
Bick John E. blacksmith, 1832 5th av
Bierman Henry, planing mill, 3 t av b 11th and 12th sts,
   res 1419 4th av
Bierman J. H. builder, 1113 3d av, res s s 4th av b 14th
   and 15th
Biern & Friedman (E. B. & C. F.) dry goods and notions,
   928 3d ave
Biern E. (B. & Friedman) res 4th av and 9th st
Biernbaum J. merchant. 1947 3d av, res same
Biggs Miss C. G. 31 Buffington Row
Biggs & Herring, lumber dealers, 920 3d av
Biggs Elizabeth J. 1133 3d av
Biggs Elizabeth L. 1133 3d av
Biggs George N. President Commercial Bank, 332 9th st,
   res 1133 3d av
Biggs Laura, book agent, 31 Buffington Row
Biggs Samuel G. 1133 3d av
Biggs W. D. 1133 3d av
Biggs W. H. grocery clerk. res 31 Buffington Row
Biggs William, capitalist, 1133 3d av
Bird Sandy, brakeman, bds 414 9th
Bird W. C. hostler, 320 9th st
Bishop A. A. 1756 5th av
Bishop E. D. (Buchanan & B.) res 1016 6th av
Bishop Florence E. 1756 5th av
Bishop Miss Garnett, 1852 5th av
Bishop William, teacher, 1756 5th av
Black Mrs. I. 840 8th av
Black Rev. J. A. pastor M. E. Church, South, 1024 4th
   av, res 1028 4th av
Black L. E. grocer, 955 3d av, res 1109 6th av
Black T. P. clerk, 955 3d av, res Thorndike, W. Va.
Black William, driver, res 8 h av b 16th and 17th sts
Blackburn J. F. shoemaker, 820 3d av, res 3d av b 5th
   and 6th sts
Blackburn M. C. shoemaker, 221 10th st, res 3d av b 5th
   and 6th sts
Blackensberry William, waiter Merchants' Hotel
Blakey Mrs. Mary, 836 6th av
Blakey Beverly, barber, 951 3d av

Blanchard James E. salesman, res 807 7th av
Blanchard Joseph, butcher, res 621 12th st
Blankenship R. blacksmith, res 2d av b 8th and 9th sts
Blanton Carrie L. teacher, res 1111 6th av
Blanton Oscar S. railroad engineer, res 1111 6th av
Bloss H. W. clerk, res 1035 6th av
Boardman & Hawkins (L. S. B. & L. G. H.) plumbers,
    326 9th st
Boardman L. F. plumber, 326 9th st, res 830 7th av
Boardman L. S. (B. & Hawkins), plumber, res 830 7th av
Bobbett Frank, laborer, res alley b 3d and 4th avs and
    11th and 12th sts
Boggess Miss E. 1025 5th av
Boggess F. N. proprietor Crystal Drug Store, 1008 3d av,
    res 1025 5th av
Boggess Norman T. drug clerk, res 1025 5th av
Boggess T. M. druggist, 1008 3d av, res 1025 5th av
Boggs Mary, 1140 4th av
Boggs Mollie, cook, 1140 4th av
Boggs W. A. carpenter, 831 7th av
Boley Mrs. D. C. 802 7th av
Bon Ton Theatre, John S. Farr & Co. prop., 935 3d av
Booker John A. 419 11th st alley
Booker Lucy, 419 11th st alley
Booker Mickey, domestic, 922 6th av alley
Boone Annie M. 738 4th av
Boone J. D. P. clerk Bank of Huntington, res 738 4th av
Boone J. W. Chief Fire Department, res 738 4th av
Booth D. W. laborer, res 9 Buffington Row
Booth James F. laborer, res 9 Buffington Row
Booth J. P. laborer, res 9 Buffington Row
Booth Martin, moulder, 909 2 av
Booth N. D. laborer, res 9 Buffington Row
Bornheim Moses, barkeeper Florentine Hotel, res 1127
    6th av
Boss Fannie, domestic, 6th av b. 9th and 10th sts
Bossinger Ernest L. 1229 3d av
Bossinger H. C. master car builder C. & O. shops, res
    1229 3d av
BOUGHNER A. BROWN, City Editor Daily Ad-
    vertiser, res 919 3d av
Bowden Christopher, laborer, res 1937 Maple av alley
Bowden Stuart, carpenter, res 1928 4th av
Bowden William, policeman, res 1933 4th av

Bowen E. A. barkeeper, res 916 5th av
Bowen Edward, clerk, bds 916 5th av
Bowen Elba, huckster, res 1932 Locust av
Bowen French (Lester & Co.)
Bowen George W. teamstar, res 1423 4th av
Bowen Hugh (Davis & B.) butcher, 749 3d av, res cor 7th
  av and 8th st
Bowen James, 12 Beardsley Row
Bowen Jefferson (Lester & Co.), restaurant, 834 3d av,
  res Davis Creek
Bowen Paris, clerk, res 915 5th av
Bowen Robert (Lester & Co.) 834 3d
Bowen W. F. moulder, res 1927 Maple av
Bowls Caroline, 2 Buffington Row
Bowser Susan E. 1946 College av
Bowyer Philip, teamster, res 1933 4th av
Boxley C. A. (B. & Frampton), res 754 3d av
Boxley & Frampton (C. A. B. & D. W. F.) grocers, 756
  3d av
Boyd Andrew, teamster, res 1119 4th av alley
Boyd Dora, 1119 4th av alley
Boyd W. P. machinist, 2217 3d av
Boyd William J. blacksmith, res 1931 4th av
Boyer F. D. butcher, res 947 4th av
Boyer Fannie N. 947 4th av
Boyer Minnie D. teacher, res 947 4th av
Brackman Robert, painter, res 422 17th st
Bradshaw Albert, servant, 1037 4th av
Bradshaw Albert, porter, 1009 3d av
Bradshaw Ida, 419 11th st alley
Brady & Werninger, grocers, 1111 3d av
Brady Bridget, 317 12th st
Brady H. J. (B. & Werninger), grocer, res 317 12 st
Brady P. S. machinist, res 317 12th st
Brady W. F. grocery clerk, res 317 12th st
Bragg James H. merchant, 824 3d av
Brammer George, 1948 Locust av
Brammer Henry, laborer, res 1926 6th av
Brammer Jackson, laborer, res 4 n Ensign shops
Brammer James M. blacksmith, 1916 8th av
Brammer Rowland, laborer, 1948 Locust av
Brammer Thomas, wks Ensign Co. bds 2413 1st av
Brandburg J. machinist, bds 1829 3d av
Brassfield Christina, laundress, 1040 3d av alley

Brassfield Gus, driver, 1043 3d av alley
Bryson Isaac, steamboat captain (retired), 1013 4'h av
Bryson Mrs. L. B. portrait artist, res 1013 4th av
Briggs Alice, 1720 4th av
Briggs Delbert, carpenter, res 1820 5th av
Briggs H. blacksmith, res 1720 4th av
Brock Henry, laborer, res 406 9th st
Brock William H. cook Florentine Hotel, res 1117 4th av
Brockley Daniel (Northcott & B.) tailor, b ls Merchants'
    Hotel
Brockmeyer A. clerk, res 1513 3d av
Brockmeyer Amelia, 1513 3d av
Brockmeyer Mrs. Clarice, book-keeper, 1042 3d av, res
    1213 3d av
Brockmeyer W. F. manager Singer Machine Co. office,
    1042 3d av, res 1513 3d av
Broh Brothers, clothiers, 901 3d av
Broh J. merchant, 901 3d av, rms 946 4th av
Broh Mike, merchant, 901 3d av, res 946 4th av
Brooks J. C. carpenter, res 2115 3d av
Brooks Joe, porter, Carrollton Hotel, 706 9th st
Brooks R. H. carpenter, res 2115 3d av
Brooks Will E. blacksmith, res 2115 3d av
Broton William T. student, res 916 5th av
Broomhall George, car builder, 1714 4th av
Broomhall Lottie, 1714 4th av
Brown Cora, 1931 Buffington av
Brown Ed, teamster, res alley b 7th and 8th sts and 3d
    and 4th avs
Brown Elsie, laborer, res 1140 4th av
Brown George, waiter; res 941 3d av
Brown Miss Ida, res 1110 7th av
Brown J. G. fireman, 1110 7th av
Brown J. P. barber, res 7th st b 2d and 3d avs
Brown James A. laborer, 213 8th st
Brown John N. carpenter, 2251 8th av
Brown Katie Mrs. 713 alley, b 7th and 8th sts and 3d and
    4th avs
Brown Laura, 713 alley b 7th and 8th and 3d and 4th avs
Brown Lena, 1938 Buffington av
Brown Leon G. building emporium, 821 3d av, res 817
    4th av
Brown Mrs. Lucy H. 817 4th av
Brown May, 12 Brick Row

Brown Minnie, 1938 Buffington av
Brown Mordecai, millwright, res 12 Brick Row
Brown Nannie, 713 alley b 3 and 4th avs and 7th and 8th
Brown Norah, 2251 8th av
Brown Napoleon, laborer, 1951 Locust av
Brown Philip, barber, 838 3d av, res 4th av b 8th and 9th
Brown Richard, car builder, bds 1829 3d av
Brown Robert G. blacksmith, res 1853 3d av
Brown S. K. engineer, res 1110 7th ave
Brown Thomas, blacksmith, res 1938 Buffington Row
Brown William, cook, alley b 2d and 3d avs and 12th and
     13th sts
Brownrigg Bros. (J. J & W. H. B.) butchers, 1055 3d av
Brownrigg J. J. (B. Bros.) res 1939 3d av
Brownrigg Jane E. 1939 3d
Brownrigg Mary E. 1939 3d av
Brownrigg Wm. H. (B. Bros.) res 1939 3d av
Brownson H. wood turner, res 6th av b 7th and 8th sts
Brunan, J. W. barber, 9th st b 4th and 5th avs, bds Con-
     tinental Hotel
Bruning Albert, shoe dealer, 3244 9th st, res same
Bruning G. A. shoe dealer, 3243 9th st, res same
Brunon F. J. barber, 308 9th st
Bryan A. W. laborer, res 1920 Locust av
Bryan T. A. attorney, 910 3d av, res West Huntington
Bryan William, bar tender, res 4th av b 8th and 9th sts
Bryant Eliza, 1731 8th av
Bryant I. V. pastor Colored Baptist Church, 1731 8th av
Bryant Mrs. Malinda, 1934 Maple av
Bryant Mrs. Susan, 1854 4th av
Buchanan & Bishop (J. E. B. & E. D. B.) piano and mu-
     sic dealers, 401 9th st
Buchanan E. D. music dealer, 401 9th st, res 1016 6th av
Buchanan J. E. (B. & Bishop), res 1016 6th av
Buck Charles, blacksmith, res 318 18th st
Buck Thomas, grocery clerk, res 7th av b 9th and 10th
Buckingham John, waiter, 941 3d av
Buffington Dr. E. S. (B. & Pritchard), physician and
     surgeon, 948 3d av, res 1235 3d av
Buffington Florence, 1303 3d av
Buffington Garland (B., McCoy & Co.) res 1201 3d av
Buffington Juliet, 1222 3d ave
Buffington Mrs. L. G. 1222 3d av

Buffington, McCoy & Co. (G. B. & S. E. McC.) boots and
    shoes, 938 3d av
Buffington & Pritchard (E. S. B. & T. J. P.) physicians,
    948 3d av
Buffington P. C. (Northcott & B.) 1222 3d av
Bull E. S livery stable, 212 9th, res 915 6th av
Bull Lelia A. 915 6th av
Bull W. H. & Son, livery stable, 212 9th st
Bull W. H. (W. H. B. & Son), res 915 6th av
Bullock T. J. engineer, res 533 10th st
Bullock Mrs. T. J. 533 10th st
Bumgardner Frank, car builder, res 108 24th st
Bumgardner Gertie; 1522 3d av
Bunch Eva, cor 2d av and 30th st
Bunch John, cor 2d av and 30th st
Bunch V. A. cor 2d av and 30th st
Bundy Harriet, 4 Buffington Row
Bundy T. E. jeweler, 908 3d av, res 1042 4th av
Bunn B. B. carpenter, 419 11th
Burchell Wm. machinist, res 5 Brick Row
Burd Winston, laborer, res 1954 6th av
Burdick Clara, 919 3d av
Burdick Mrs. M. A. 919 3d av
Burgess F. C. core maker, res 1706 4th av
Burgess Jackson, laborer, res 1746 College av
Burgess Melissa, 1746 College av
Burgess Sarah, 1746 College av
Burk Emma, cook, res 1134 6th av
Burke Henry W. machinist, res 313 11th st
Burke John W. bar tender, res 3d av b 8th and 9th sts
Burke T. J. real estate agent, s s 2d av b 7th and 8th sts,
    bds n s 3d av b 11th and 12th sts
Burks Charles, teamster, rms 1225 3d av alley
Burk Henry, laborer, 1951 Locust av
Burks Ida L. res river b 25th and 26th sts
Burks John, brakeman, bds 1727 8th av
Burks L. H. Director First National Bank, res river b
    25th and 26th sts
Burks Lulu, res river b 25th and 26th sts
Burks Mary C. res river b 25th and 26th sts
Burks William, waiter, alley b 2d and 3d avs and 7th and
    8th sts
Burkheimer Martin, foreman blacksmith, res 1204 4th av
Burkheimer W. M. blacksmith, res 1204 4th av

Burnes Albert. blacksmith, res 326 18th st
Burnes Charles E. engineer, res 326 18th st
Burnes Elizabeth, clerk, res 1121 3d av
Burnes Ella, clerk, res 1121 3d av
Burnes Homer S. machinist, 1121 3d av
Burnes Ingaba, 1121 3d av
Burnes J. A. restaurant and grocery, 3d av b 8th and 9th, res same
Burnes J. T. printer, res 326 18th st
Burnett J. W. insurance agent, 409 9th st, res 7th av b 9th and 10th
Burns Anna, 736 6th av
Burns C. E. engineer, res e s 18th st b 3d and 4th avs
Burns F. L. engineer, res 736 6th av
Burns John Jr. bridge builder. res 633 6th av
Burns Katharine, 736 6th av
Burns W. A. 736 6th av
Burnside William, blacksmith. res 1951 4th av
Burrows Dan, teamster, 1955 Virginia av
Bush F. D. bar keeper Merchants'. Hotel, res cor 2d av and 9th st
Bush Fred, clerk, 925 3d av
Busicok G. L. grocery clerk, res 1109 6th av
Butler B. F. 828 6th av
Butler C. H. fireman, res 828 6th av
Butler H. C. bar keeper, bds Merchants' Hotel
Butler Hattie, 828 6th av
BUTLER & KEYS, Tonsorial Artists, 929 3d av
Butler Moses, barber, 929 3d av, res 213 14th st
Byron William, bar keeper, res 847 4th av

C

Cairns J. saloon keeper, 3d av b 9th and 10th sts, bds 1038 4th av

Caldwell Ida. B. res 1141 3d av

Caldwell J. L. banker, 3d av b 9th and 10th sts, res 1141 3d av

Caldwell Ouida, res 1141 3d av

Calhoun F. M. manuf of medicines, 417 11th st, res same

Calhoun John C. clerk, res 417 11th st

Calhoun Mrs. M. A. res 417 11th st

Calhoun Miss M. B. 417 11th st

Calhoun Walter E. clerk, res 417 11th st

Call Sarah, res 1849 4th av

Callaghan Peter Jr., res 1736 College av

Callaghan Peter Sr., res 1736 College av

Calloway Mrs. Emily, res 832 3d av

Calloway John, laborer, bds 832 3d av

Calloway Wm. laborer, bds 832 3d av

Cally J. M. hostler, res 727 alley b 2d and 3d avs and 7th and 8th sts

Camden John T. section foremam, res 1919 Maple av

Cammack Chas. W. clerk First Nat Bank, res 1522 3d av

CAMMACK J. H. Insurance and Real Estate Agent, 9th st b 3d and 4th avs, res 1522 3d av

Cammack T. H. student, res 1522 3d av

Cammack Mrs. M. J. res 1522 3d av

Campbell Eugene M. traveling salesman, res 1244 4th av

Campbell & Holt, (C. W. C. & T. J. H.), attorneys at law, 856 Ward Block.

Campbell C. W. (C. & Holt), attorney, 856 3d av, res cor 7th av and 8th st

Campbell C. W. attorney at law, 223 9th st. res 1134 6th av

CAMPBELL EUGENE M. President Huntington Printing and Publishing Co., 308 10th st, res 1244 4th av

Campbell Capt. J. T. steamboat captain, res 1240 3d av

Canterberry Lizzie, domestic, res 703 5th av

Cantrell Chas. molder, res 1851 8th av

CARDER Dr. A. S. dentist, 903 3d av, res 3d av b 9th and 10th sts

Cardwell Henry, blacksmith, res 619 20th st

Cardwell Wm. teamster, 913 4th av

Cardwell M. laborer, res 817 4th av alley

DR. A. S CARDER

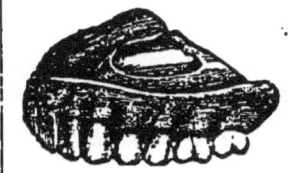

DENTIST.

HAS MOVED HIS DENTAL OFFICE TO

BROH'S NEW BLOCK,

Cor. Third Av. and Ninth St.

Where he will be found at all hours. If you want first-class work give him a call.

Carey W. E. grocery clerk, res s s 8th av, b 8th and 9th sts
Carnahan A. J. fireman, bds 2 Frame Row
Carpenter Ed. laborer, res 2325 8th av
Carr Quincey, machine hand, bds 1245 3d av
Carr Thos. M. carpenter, res 1113 4th av
Carr W. U. conductor, res 817 7th av
Carrico John, car inspector, res 1509 R. R. b 15th and 16th sts
Carroll Bertha, res 1008 4th av
Carroll Emily, res 1046 4th av
Carroll Harry, hotel clerk, s e cor 4th av and 9th st, res 1046 4th av
Carroll Mrs. J. C. res 1008 4th av
Carroll J. C. carpenter, res 1008 4th av
Carroll Maggie, 1008 4th av
CARROLLTON HOTEL, Goodwin & Poindexter, props. opp C. & O. depot
Carry Luella, res 826 8th av
Carry Mrs. Maria, res 826 8th av
Carry Willie, clerk, res 816 8th av

Carson Geo. laborer, res 1942 7th av

Cart J. F. car builder, res 2209½ 3d av

Carter Cora A. res 741 alley b 7th and 8th sts, and 3d and 4th avs

Carter Dr. D. P. dentist, 913½ 3d av, res 1011 3d av

Carter H. L. brakeman, res 814 7th av

Carter Henry, teamster, res 1831 Virginia av

Carter Henry, carpenter, res 1953 Buffington av

Carter J. B. carpenter, res 1142 4th av

Carter J. C. carpenter, res 1953 Buffington av

Carter John H. laborer, res 1949 Locust av

Carter Mrs. Lena, res 1041 5th av

Carter Lillie, res 1142 4th av

Carter Mrs. Mary, laundress, res 741 alley b 7th and 8th sts, and 3d and 4th avs

Carter Virginia, res 741 alley b 7th and 8th sts, and 3d and 4th avs

Carter W. L. machinist, res 814 7th av

Cartman Mrs. Mary, laundress, res 1752 4th av

Caruthers Wm. telegraph operator, res 529 12th st

Caverlee Frank T. blacksmith, res 1338 3d av

Caverlee Mrs. Zuba A. 1338 3d av

Cartwright Thomas, res 1023 14th st

Cartwright Wm. heater, res 1023 14th st

Cash Geo. laborer, res 316 11th st

Cash Rhoda, res 316 11th st

Cooper G. J. harness maker, bds 736 4th av

Carper C. B. carpenter, res 2024 4th av

Carper Lucius, res 2024 4th av

Carper Stanley, res 2024 4th av

Cassidey Bella, cook, at depot

Cassler Gracie, res n s 4th av West Huntington

Cassler John, supt H. E. L. Co. 927 4th av, res West Huntington

Cottle C. W. farmer, res s s 5th av b 5th and 6th sts

Cottle Mrs. V. B. res s s 5th av, b 5th and 6th sts

Central Land Co. office 851 3d av

Chaffin Wm. jeweler, 2011 3d av, res same

Chaffin W. B. & Sons, jewelers, 2011 3d av

Chaffins Arthur, hostler, bds 725 3d av

Chambers Bertha, res 1509 3d av

Chambers Bettie, res 1840 8th av

Chambers Ernest, machinist, res 1509 3d av

Chambers Harry, pattern maker, res 1509 3d av

Chambers J. B. coal dealer, cor 16th st and 3d av, res 1548 3d av

Chambers John, machinist, res 1509 3d av

Chambers John W. carpenter, res 1840 8th av

Chambers Norah G. res 1840 8th av

Chambers Mrs. Patrick, res 1548 3d av

Chambers W. A. machinist, res 1840 8th av

Chandler Ellen, res 11 Beardsley Row

Chandler James, laborer, res 11 Beardsley Row

Chapman C. A. carpenter, res 1852 8th av

Chapman C. E. pipe fitter, res 1810 4th av

Chapman E. F. insurance agent, 217 10th st, res West Huntington

Chapman Hattie, servant, res 946 4th av

Chapman Hattie, 1136 3d av

Chapman Henry, blacksmith, res alley b 3d and 4th avs, and 11th and 12th sts

Chapman Ida, res 819 6th av

Chapman Jas. carpenter, res 1810 4th av

Chapman Jennie, cook, rms 1215 3d av alley

Chapman Jennie, cook, res 524 11th st

Chapman Louise, res alley b 3d and 4th avs, and 11th and 12th sts

Chapman Lee, domestic, res 1005 6th av

Chapman Malinda, res alley b 3d and 4th avs, and 11th and 12th sts

Chapman R. 1322 n 3d av

Chapman Seymour, carpenter, res 1828 Virginia av

Chapman Stonewall, bar tender, bds 916 5th av

Chappell Lewis, night watchman, 838 7th av

Cheatham W. F. compositor, rms 12st st and 4th av

Cheesman Dr. A. M. Physician, res 2410 2d av

Cheesman Miss M. M. res 2410 2d av

Cheshire C. A. pattern maker, res 1219 6th av

Cheterman W. F. printer, res 1125 4th av

Chick Ed. laborer, bds 1941 Buffington av

Childers Chas. laborer, res 1818 5th av

Childers Jack, clerk, res 1728 4th av

Childers John B. res 14 Buffington Row

Childers Bettie J. res 1854 5th av

Childers Emma, res 1854 5th av

Childers Mamie, res 1854 5th av

Childrey H. T. policeman, res 842 4th av

Childrey J. H. laborer, res 842 4th av

Childrey Jesse, laborer, res 3d av b 8th and 9th sts
Childrey John, laborer, res 3d av b 8th and 9th sts
Childrey Wm. L. teamster, res 842 4th av
• Chin Lonis, teamster, res n s 3d av West Huntington
Christian Jas. A. carpenter, res 1825 Virginia av
Christy J. C. machinist, res 1846 8th av
Christy Jeff, axle turner, res n 24th st
Christian L. J. car inspector, res 1507 R. R.
Clair Joseph, machinist, res 725 6th av
Clapper Hanson, telegraph operator, res 1921 3d av
Clark A. M. & Co , shoe store, 956 3d av
Clark A. M. (A. M. C & Co.) shoe dealer, 956 3d av and
    223 10th st, res 1336 4th av
Clark A. M. constable and U. S. deputy marshal, 910 3d
    av, res 541 10th st
Clark Cynthia, res 317 9th st
Clark Ed. news agent, bds 721 3d av
Clark J. W. brakeman, res 1011 4th av
Clark Mrs. Maggie, res 523 10th st
Clark Mrs. Mattie, res 1011 4th av
Clark S. M. res 1336 4th av
Clark Silas, sawyer, res 4th av b 13th and 14th sts
Clark Thomas, res 4th av b 13th and 14th sts
Clark Willie, waiter, Merchants' Hotel
Clay H. prop Southern News Co., res C & O depot
Clay Thomas H. clerk, res 935 7th av
Clemments William, engineer, res 1028 7th av
Clendenin William, engineer, bds 818 4th av
Cleveland Albert, brakeman, bds 719 alley b 2d and 3d
    avs, and 7th and 8th sts
Cleveland C. R. express messenger, bds 641 5th av
Close J. H. carpenter, res 1208 3d av
Clouston R. M. merchandise broker, 856 3d av, res 1322
    6th av
C. & O. Repair Shops. William Hassman, M. M.; W.
    J. Gunn, Chief Clerk ; H. C. Bossinger, Master Car
    Builder; John Taylor, General Fereman ; R. C.
    Ward, Foreman Smith Shop ; W. W. Points, Fore-
    man Round House ; J. A. Gohen, Foreman Painter ;
    George F Hall, Foreman Tinner ; J. D. Graves,
    Foreman Boiler Maker ; H. F. Rosenstul, Foreman
    Freight Depot: E. J. Davis, Foreman Passenger Car
    Dep't ; J. B. Miles, Shipping Clerk.
Cobb Jos. laborer, res 1694 9th st

Cobb Mary, res 1694 9th av
Cobb Melvin, bds 1905 Buffington av
Cockrell John M. car builder, res 1719 Virginia av
Cody Patrick, lineman, res 1105 3d av alley
Coe John, engineer, res 618 10th st
Coffman J. W. car builder, res 1246 3d av
Coffman Robt E. L. car builder, bds 2113 3d av
Coghill J. A. saloon keeper, cor 3d av and 8th st, res same
Cohen C. jeweler, 908 3d av, res 1036 4th av
Cole C. C. tinner, 3d av b 10th and 11 sts, res 1025 7th av
Cole C. F. plumber, 1115 3d av
Cole Charles, tinner, 1033 3d av, res s 7th av b 10th and
    11th sts
Cole E. R. carpenter, bds 753 2d av
Cole E. R. bottler and mixer, 947 2d av, res_s s 2d av
    n 8th st
Cole Elias laborer, bds 1956 4th av
Coles Edward, laborer, res 9 Beardsley Row
Cole Thomas H. laborer, res 1117 4th av alley
Cole Zara, bds 753 2d av
Collier Rev. J. L. res 520 9th st parsonage
Collins Allen, teamster, res 1937 Maple av alley
Collins E. C. car builder, res 1425 4th av
Collins Mary, res 7 n Ensign Shops
Collins Thomas, laborer, res 7 n Ensign Shops
Colten James, painter, bds 808 4th av
Combs Charles, drug clerk, 3d av b 10th and 11th sts
Comer Annie W. 1128 3d av
Comer Mrs. H. W. 1128 3d av
Comer Mertie, 101 24th st
Comings Benjamin, jeweler, 1013 3d av, res 1038 4th av
COMMERCIAL BANK, George N. Biggs, President :
    W. B. Prickitt, Cashier, 332 9th st
Comston J. D. carpenter, 1818 4th av
Conard T. F. baggage master C. & O. 925 6th av
Conerton Thomas, tailor, 1053 3d av, res n w cor 4th av
    and 11th st
Conley E. M. car painter, 1107 6th av
Connelly Everett, painter, rms 1344 6th av
Connolly Martin, merchant, 2327 8th av, res 2325 8th av
Conrad Mary, laundress, 1117 4th av alley
Continental Hotel, Harvey Adkins, mgr, cor 2d av and
    8th st
Cook Grace C. compositor, 9th st b 6th and 7th avs

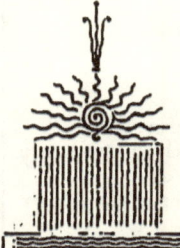

OFFICERS . . . .

G. N. BIGGS, President.
F. F. McCULLOUGH, Vice-Pres't.
W. B. PRICKITT, Cashier.

✳ COMMERCIAL ✳

BANK

—OF—

HUNTINGTON, W. VA.

Cor. Ninth St. & Fourth Av.

OPP. P. O. BUILDING.

Transacts a Legitimate Banking Business in all its Branches.
Sells Foreign Exchange.

CAPITAL,   -   *$50,000.00*

DIRECTORS . . . . . .

G. N. Biggs.	W. T. Thompson.
F. F. McCullough.	W. B. Prickitt.
D. E. Abbott.	H. M. Ensign
W. J. Parsons.	Rufus Switzer.

Chapman Fry.

Coon John, express messenger, 529 12th st
Coon Henry, wks Ensign Co, res n 24th st
Cooper J. W. wks Ensign Co, res 2109 3d av
Cooper Martha, 6 Beardsley Row
Cooper Sarah 2109 3d av
Core Sarah, domestic, 1204 3d av
Core W. H. car builder, 613 20th st
Corlin John, blacksmith, 1105 3d av alley
Coverson Fanny, 808 4th av
Cottle Mrs. Lena, 2217 3d av
Cottle I. E. machinist, 1925 6th av
Cottle Walter J. laborer, 1951 5th av
Coverson Perry, shoe maker, cor 10th st and 3d av, bds
    808 4th av
Cox A. E. merchant, 2213 3d av, res same
Cox Alvin, telegraph operator, res 725 6th av
Cox Dora, domestic, 918 4th av
Cox Dr. E. W. physician, 1837 3d av, res same
Cox Gypsie, bds 733 2d av
Cox M. C. car builder, 1919 Buffington av
Cox Sally, domestic, res 1047 4th av
Coy T. H. engineer, 1841 3d av
Cox W. B. solicitor and book agent, bds Huntington Hotel
Craig John, 14th st b 2d and 3 av alley
Craven Thomas, fireman, 910 5th av
Crowder Mary, domestic, 5th av b 10th and 11th sts
Crawford Anna, 729 alley b 6th and 7th avs
Crawford F. M. laborer, 618 9th st
Crawford Wyatt, conductor, C. & O. R. R. 1031 7th av
Creekbaum J. T. carpenter, 1219 3d av
Crider Jacob L. druggist, 1034 3d av, res 414 11th st
Crider Levi, book seller and stationer, 1011 3d av, res s e
    cor 6th av and 10th st
Crider Mrs. J. L. cor 4th av and 11th st
Crissinger Irvin, motor man, bds 2413 1st av
Critzer Grant, carpenter, 1221 3d av
Crooks Clara, 2106 4th av
Crow Beatrice, 1049 4th av
Crystal Mary, 1835 4th av
Cullen Edward, clerk, 4th av b 10th and 11th sts
Cullen George, Assistant Street Commissioner, 1015 4th av
Cullen George, Jr. fireman, 1015 4th av
Cullen Harry, clerk, 1015 4th av
Cummins Albert, s s 3d av, West Huntington

22	HUNTINGTON [DAV] DIRECTORY.

Cummins Joseph, farmer, s s 3d av, West Huntington
Cummins Londas, laborer, s s 3d av, West Huntington
Cummins William, s s 3d av, West Huntington
Cundiff Isaac, fireman, 617½ 19th st
Cunningham Corum, wks C. & O. shops, res 1843 8th av
Cunningham J. F. conductor, res 1122 6th av
Cunningham James R. machinist, res 1843 8th av
Cunningham Jane, 1843 8th av
Cunningham Mary, 1843 8th av
Cunningham Mary M. domestic, 523 10th st
Cunningham Melissa, 1843 8th av
Cunningham William 1843 8th av
Curry Charles, patern maker, res 1924 8th av
Curry Robert, laborer, res 1924 8th av
Curtis Jesse, carpenter, res 1698 8th av
Curtis W. G. laborer, res 1698 8th av
Curtright Logan, brakeman, res 721 3d av

D

Daily John, merchant tailor, bds Merchants' Hotel
Daily J. P. tailor, bds cor 2d av and 9th st
Damron J. R. salesman, 1129 4th av
Damron Mrs. L. D. 1129 4th av
Damewood Charles, breakman, 529 12th st
Danford Cordelia, 1913 5th av
Danford William, carpenter, 1913 5th av
Daniels Charles, waiter, 941 3d av
Daniel Ella, 753 4th av
Dartt Allen J. car builder, 1743 4th av
Daub William F. moulder, bds 1245 3d av
Davenport William, hod carrier, 1515 3d av alley
Davies Mrs. Ann, 1035 4th av
Davies Annie M. music teacher, 520 7th st
Davies Benjamin L. machinist, 1035 4th av
Davies Mrs. E. F. 520 7th st
Davies E. J. foreman coach dep't, C. & O. R. R. 1035 4th av
Davies John, carpenter and vocal music teacher, 520 7th st
Davies J. L. carpenter, 520 7th st
Davies R. B. telegraph operator, 520 7th st
Davies Thomas C. 1035 4th av

Davis Dr. A. G. (Hallenhan & D.), physician, 823 3 av
Davis America, Virginia House, 2d av
Davis Anna, stewardess, 941 3d av
Davis Anna A. 316 10th st
Davis B. T. druggist, 801 3d av, res 1128 3d av
Davis & Bowen, (V. B. D. & H. B.) meat market, 749 and 751 3d av
Davis Mrs. Celest C. 1128 3d av
Davis Charles, car builder, 1806 5th av
Davis Mrs. C. F. Virginia House, 2d av
Davis Rev. E. A. minister, Huntington Circuit, res 1812 4th av
Davis G. A. trader, 1939 4th av
Davis Gallaher, machine hand, 1939 Locust av
Davis H. A. lumber inspector, 1812 4th av
Davis J. B. butcher, 1905 3d av, res same
Davis J. S. grocer, 1955 Locust av, res 717 20th st
Davis J. V. clerk, 1003 7th av
Davis Jefferson, butcher, 1905 3d av, res 1917 3d av
Davis John L. building and loan agent, 1904 Locust av
Davis Flora, Virginia House, 2d av
Davis George W. painter, 721 4th av
Davis Gordon, office boy Herald, 316 10 st
Davis Harry, 416 e 8th st
Davis John, express messenger, Adams Express Company, 641 5th av
Davis Lelia, cook, 941 3d av
Davis Louis, domestic, 1303 3d av
Davis Margret, cook, 1219 6th av
Davis Moey, 926 7th av
Davis Mrs. Mary A. 1738 8th av
Davis Mrs. Mary A. 1216 7th av
Davis Mary E. 316 10th st
Davis Maurice, bartender, 406 9th st
Davis Ottis, (Lester & Co.) 3d av b 8th and 9th sts, bds cor 4th av and 9th st
Davis R. C. pattern maker, 316 10th st
Davis R. H. carpenter, 5th av b 9th and 19th sts
Davis R. H. mechanic, 1016 6th av alley
Davis Robert L. printer, 721 4th av
Davis Samuel T. 721 4th av
Davis Thomas, stone cutter, 808 4th av
Davis V. B (D & Bowen), butcher, 749 and 751 3d av, res Buck Fork

Davis Thomas, laborer, bds 213 w 8th st
Davis W. W. laborer, 1942 7th av
Davis Walter, butcher, 3d av b 7th and 8th sts, bds 916 5th av
Davis Walter, (Lester & Co.) 3d av b 8th and 9th sts, bds 916 5th av
Davis William, conductor, C. & O. R. R. rms 636 10th st
Davis William A. carpenter, 1125 4th av
Davis William, conductor, 926 7th av
Davis William A. carpenter, 1035 4th av
Dawkins L. D. clerk, Guyandotte
Dawson Anna, chambermaid, 941 3d av
Dawson Lewis, carpenter, 615 20th st
Dawson Martin L. wks plaster factory, 14th st alley b 2d and 3d av
Dawson Mrs Emma R. 14th st b 2d and 3d av
Dawson F. M. car builder, 1833 8th av
Dawson Rev. G. K. minister, Second Huntington Charge, 1833 8th av
Dawson George, carpenter, 17 Buffington Row
Dawson Theodore W. car builder, 1932 6th av
Day G. H. foreman Ensign Co. 116 24th st
Day James A. laborer, n 24th st
Day J. R. plumber 1115 3d av, res 1135 4th av
Day R. L book-keeper, 6th av, West Huntington
Day Mrs. Sarah, cook, 1125 3d av
Deacon Alonzo, wks Ensign Co. bds 1946 College av
Dean Dr. T. H. physician, 527 10th st
Dean Thomas M. 1740 5th av
DeBard M. moulder, 1804 4th av
Decker J. A. carpenter and restaurant, 320¼ 9th st, res same
Decker Laura, 320¼ 9th st
Decker Martha A. caterer, 320¼ 9th st
Deen J. E. laborer, 414 17 st
Deegans Mary, 313 19th st
Deihl Frank, grocer, 1955 3d av, res same
Deihl Lewis, 1949 3d av
DeLaughter George, watchman, C. & O. shops, 15 Frame Row
Delabar Charles, 737 and 739 3d av
Delabar Carrie, 737 and 739 3d av
Delabar Jennie, 737 and 739 3d av
Delabar K. shoemaker, 856 8th av, res 737 3d av

Dempsey Mrs. M. E. dressmaker, 1039 3d av, res same
Dempsey S. P. frame maker, n e cor 4th av and 9th st, res 1039 3d av
Denny Mrs. Emma, 823 3d av
Denny Zach. painter and contractor, 823 3d av, res same
Derbyshire Miss C. M. 1456 6th av
Derbyshire H. J. Sr. brass moulder, 1456 6th av
Derbyshire H. J. Jr. machinist, 1456 6th av alley
Derbyshire T. G. brass moulder, 1456 6th av alley
Detherage Wiley, forge hand, bds 101 24 st
Dew W. A. clerk, Adams Express Co. n w cor 7th av and 10th st
Dey Mrs. Fannie, seamstress, s s 3d av b 10th and 11th sts
Dick M. F. carpenter, 2211½ 3d av
Dickens Capt. John, plasterer, 1116 4th av
Dickens Robert, plasterer, 1116 4th av
Dickey Allie, 1811 3d av
Dickey Bessie, 1704 4th av
Dickey Dora, dressmaker, 324 9th st, res 1811 3d av
Dickey Fannie, forelady knitting factory, 1811 3d av
Dickey Frank, saw mill, 1920 4th av
Dickey George, engineer, 1811 3d av
Dickey Hamilton, undertaker, 944 3d av, res 942 3d av
Dickey J. C. book-keeper, 944 4th av
Dickey J. L. carpenter, res 1704 4th av
Dickey Lulu, clerk, res 1811 3d av
Dickey Wealthy, res 1704 4th av
Dickey Wm. laborer, res 1811 3d av
Dickson P. Byron, delivery clerk, res 701 5th av
Dickson Capt. J. G. agent Gerke Brewing Co. Cincinnati, 10th st saloon, res 701 and 703 5th av
Dickson Mrs. M. S. res 701 and 703 5th av
Dickerson R. B. chief dispatcher C. & O. R. R. bds 1012 6th av
Diehl Albert, carpenter, res 2319 8th av
Diehl Lizzie, nurse, res 1037 4th av
Diehl Robert, saloonist, 3d av and 20th st, res 2007 3d av
Dill Tony, teamster, res s s alley b 6th and 7th avs and 9th and 10th sts
Dillon John, fireman, bds 1 Brick Row
Dillon John M. blacksmith, res 1928 6th av
Dillon Mary, chambermaid, res 406 9th
DIMMICK M. C. cashier First Nat Bank, res 914 6th av
Dinsler Miss L. M. res 1917 3d av

Divers Laura, servant, 1312 4th av
Doolittle E. S. attorney, 910 3d av
Doolittle Frank L. secretary and treasurer Belt Line R. R.
   res 624 10th st
Dorsey Thos. carpenter, res e s 8th av
Dotson Chas. car builder, bds 101 24th st
Dotson F. C. carpenter, res 1832 4th av
Douthit E. F. harness maker, res 736 4th av
Douthit Edward Sr., (D. & Leist), saddlery and harness,
   407 w 9th st, res 4th av b 7th and 8th sts
Douthit & Leist, (E. F. D. & A. L. L.), dealers in sad-
   dles and harness, 407 9th st
Downer Mrs. C. C. res 916 7th av
Downer Janie, student, res 916 7th av
Douthit Mrs. Lizzie, res 736 4th av
Downey Adalia, res 2335 8th av
Downey Ella, res 2335 8th av
Downey John, saloon keeper 1901 3d av, res same
Downey Jennie, res 823 6th av
Downey Mary, res 2335 8th av
Downey Tom, carpenter and wagon maker, res 2335 8th av
Doyle C. C. ticket agent C. & O. depot, res 724 6th av
Doyle Carl, barber, bds 727 6th av
Doyle J. T. machinist, res 1346 4th av
Doyle Jas. carpenter, C. & O. shop
Drake W. F. carpenter, res 739 alley b 7th and 8th sts and
   4th and 5th avs
Dresher Belle, tailoress, res 1338 3d av
Dresher J. F. car builder, res 1142 4th av
Dresher Tena, seamstress, bds 3d av b 13th and 14th sts
Dresher Lena, tailoress, bds 1338 3d av
Driggs Benjamin, clerk, 918 6th av
Drown John P. assistant foreman, 1901 Buffington av
Drummond L. F. carpenter, res 1825 8th av
Drummond S. T. carpenter, res 1827 8th av
Dudley P. G. clerk rms 754 3d av
DUDLEY J. R. prop Daily Times, 217 10th st. bds St.
   Nicholas Tavern
Dugan Dennis, laborer, 36 Buffington Row
Dugan J. C. porter, res cor 2d av and 9th st
Dugan Jas. H. blacksmith, res 8 Brick Row
Dugan Jos. F. machinist, res 8 Brick Row
Dugan Patrick, foreman, res 8 Brick Row
Dullunty John, blacksmith, res 1940 8th av

Duke Elizabeth, res 808 4th av
Duke John A. boarding house, 808 4th av, res same
Duke Mary, res 1023½ 6th av
Duke Thomas, horse doctor, 10th st b 3d and 4th avs, res
   1023½ 6th av
Dunilan Nora, res 710 6th av
Duncan Bida, res 1724 College av
Duncan Mrs. Hattie, res 2003 3d av
Duncan Henry laborer, res 1724 College av
Duncan Israel, railroader, res 709 10th st
Duncan John L. carpenter, res 1844 4th av
Duncan Maggie, cook, res 1109 4th av
Duncan Maggie, dress maker, res 1805 8th av
Duncan Wm. laborer, res 2003 3d av
Dunn W. W. foreman planing mill, bds 1245 3d av
Dunn J. F. conductor C. & O. R. R. res 1107 6th av
Dunshire Wm. machinist, res 2325 8th av
Durea C. E. moulder, res 1802 5th av
Durea Isaac, res 1802 5th av
Durea R. E. grocery clerk, res n w cor 18th st and 5th av
Durea R. E. teamster, res 1802 5th av
Durkin James, laborer, res 709 10th st
Dusenberry C. C. (D. & Wilson) grocer, 1001 3d av, res
   1007 3d av
Dusenberry & Wilson (C. C. D. & W. B. Wilson), grocery
   and feed store, 1001 3d av
Dusty William, teamster, 5 Beardsley Row
Dwyer Mathew F. butcher, 1055 3d av, res 1939 3d av
Dyel Edward, student, 916 5th av

E

Earl Columbia S. 1951 8th av
Earl David, teamster, 1951 8th av
Earl Franklin E. student, 1951 8th av
Earl George A. wks in C. & O. shops, 1951 8th av
Earl Lucian E. teamster, 1951 8th av
Earl W. R. fireman, 1921 8th av
Earles Charles, farmer, 1725 8th av
Earles Charles, moulder, 1721 3d av
Earles Leander, blacksmith, 1815 8th av
Earles J. R. sewing machine agent, 825½ 3d av
Earles Joseph V. moulder, 1721 3d av
Earley Belle, cook, 618 9th st

Farley James, wks C. & O. shops, 1688 8th av
Early James, waiter, cor 9th st and 2d av
Easthorn Joseph, wks Ensign Co. 20 Buffington Row
Easton Daniel, 11 Buffington Row
Eba T. M. salesman, 922 6th av alley
Eckhart Charles, teamster, 831 2d av
Edens J. D. carpenter, 751 2d av
Edmonds D. R. fish dealer, 215 10th st alley
Edmonds S. B. fish dealer, 215 10th st alley
Edwards G. B. lumber inspector, 719 6th av
Edwards R. saw mill hand, 1905 5th av
Edwards Ruth M. 719 6th av
Edwards W. T. engineer C. & O. R. R. 630 10th st
Eggleton Bonner F. 1415 R. R.
Eggleton Mrs. Emily, 21 Buffington Row
Eggleton P. M. brakeman C. & O. R. R. 1415 R. R.
Eisenmann Andy, machinist, 1436 3d av
Eisenmann Charles, jeweler, 923 3d av, res 1436 3d av
Eisenmann Josie, dress maker, 1436 3d av
Eisenmann Mary, dressmaker, 1436 3d av
Ekhart Charles, laborer, 2d av b 8th and 9th sts
Elder Mrs. Caroline, 1021 7th av
Elegar Jacob, carpenter, (City Councilman) 5th av b 8th
　　and 9th sts, res 814 6th av
Elkins William, car builder, res 923 4th av
ELLIS J. F. Treasurer Herald Co. res w 12th st b 6th
　　and 6th avs
Elliot S. G. machinist, res 825½ 3d av
Elliot W. J. mattress maker, res 943 4th av
Elliot W. P. engineer, res 1008 7th av
Ellis G. W. truck builder, res 1916 4th av
Ellis Mrs. Ellen, res 22 Buffington Row
Ellis Merton, truck builder, res 1916 4 av
Elswick Fred. clerk, rms 747 alley b 7th and 8th sts and
　　4th and 5th avs
Elswick Fred teamster, bds w s 8th st b 4th and 5th avs
Ely George S. machine adjuster, 410 e 8th st
Emmons C. D. hardware merchant, 902 and 904 3d av, res
　　e s 11th st b 5th and 6th avs
Emmons Mrs. D. W. res Pleasant View
Emmons W. D. banker, Bank of Huntington and First
　　National Bank, res Pleasant View
Emmons Elizabeth, res Pleasant View

EMMONS & MARR,

Successors to Parsons & Emmons.

Hardware and Stoves,

DOORS. SASH. GLASS AND OILS.

Manufacturers of Tinware.

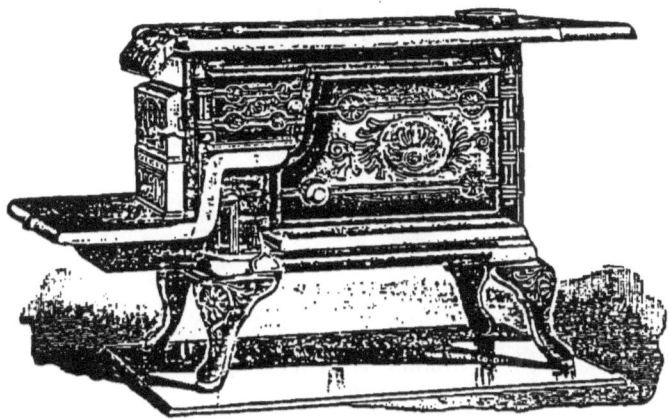

JOBBERS AND RETAILERS

— IN —

*Hardware. Stoves, Sash, Doors and
Builders' Hardware.*

We Carry the Largest and Best Selected Stock of General Hardware in the City. Agents for
**OLIVER CHILLED PLOWS. MALTA PLOWS,
WHITELY MOWERS.**

No. 902 THIRD AVENUE. Corner Ninth Street,

HUNTINGTON, W. VA.

Emmons J. A. (Johnson & E.) furniture dealer, 944 3d av
  res 9th st b 6th and 7th avs
EMMONS & MARR, Wholesale and Retail Dealers
  in Hardware, 902 and 904 3d av
Emrick Helen W. music teacher, res 727 6th av
Emrick John, painter, 727 6th av
Emrick Mabel E. 727 6th av
Emrick W. O. spring maker, 727 6th av
Engleman L. L. clerk passenger depot, res 9th st
Enochs Elisha, moulder, 4 n Ensign Shops
Ensco Jas. E. machinist, res 2045 8th av
Ensco Jas. 2045 8th av
ENSIGN E. Secretary and Treasurer Ensign Manuf Co.
  3d av b 23d and 24 sts, res 1322 3d av
Ensign H. M. foreman Ensign Co. res 1138 6th av
Ensign John W. wks Ensign Manuf Co. res 1322 3d av
ENSIGN MF'G CO. manuf of Freight Cars, Wheels,
  Journal Bearings, &c. 3d av b 23d and 24th st
Ensley A. F. blacksmith, res 1937 8th av
Ensley G. L. carpenter, res 1941 8th av
ENSLOW C. R. physician, 916 3d av, res 3d av b 13th
  and 14th sts
Enslow E. B. insurance agent, cor 9th st and 3d av,
  res 1309 3d av
Enslow Frank, lawyer, cor 10th st and 3d av, res 1303
  3d av
Enslow F. B. (Simms & E.), attorney at law, 222 10th
  st, res s e cor 3d av and 13th st
Epps Mrs. Evelina, 749 alley b 2d and 3d avs and 7th
  and 8th sts
Epps Tony, hod carrier, res 749 alley b 2d and 3d avs
  and 7th and 8th sts
Erley Nick, laborer, res 1117 4th av alley
Erskine Isaac, carpenter, res 6 Buffington av
Erskine L. apprentice C. & O. shops, res 1133 4th av
Erskine Wm. carpenter, res 1133 4th av
Erwin Geo. car builder, bds 101 24th st
Estep Carter, teamster, res 8th st b 2d and 3d av
Estie Ellis, domestic, res 1216 6th av
Esque Dyke, painter, res 30 Buffington Row
Esque Robt. machine hand, res 1931 6th av
Eureka Steam Laundry, Geo. Eversole, prop, 929 and 931
  2d av,
Evans Curtis carpenter, res 1847 3d av

THE

ENSIGN MANUFACTURING COMPANY, ∴ ∴ ∴

HUNTINGTON, W. VA.

New York Office, No. 11 Pine Street.

MANUFACTURERS OF

FREIGHT ✳ CARS

OF ALL DESCRIPTIONS,

CHILLED CAR WHEELS.

CAR AXLES, CAR CASTINGS,

JOURNAL BEARINGS,

WHEELS FITTED TO AXLES.

CAPACITY,	20 BOX CARS. ∴	DAILY.
	400 CAR WHEELS	
	80 AXLES. ∴ ∴	

F. E. CANDA, PRESIDENT. 11 Pine Street, New York.
C. J. CANDA. VICE-PRES., 11 Pine Street, New York.
J. W. SAVIN, GEN'L AGENT, 11 Pine Street, New York.
E. ENSIGN, SEC'Y & TREASURER, Huntington. W. Va.

Evans J. Thomas, res 1728 5th av

Everett Mrs. N. Principal Oley School, res 1125 3d av

Evers Cora, res 1039 3d av

EVERS PAUL, painter, 10th st b 3d and 4th avs, res 1039 3d av

Eversole Geo. prop Eureka Steam Laundry, 929 2d av, res 5th av b 9th and 10th sts

Eversole Geo. T. driver, res 5th av b 9th and 10th sts

F

Falkner Letha, domestic, Marshall College

Falkner Mattie, domestic, Marshall College

Falls G. W. carpenter, res 1814 5th av

Falwell William W. laborer, cor 2d av and 30th st

Farmer John, laborer, res n 24th av

Farr J. A. res 841 4th av

Farr John S. saloon keeper, 935 3d av, res 841 s 4th av

Farr John S. & Co. prop. Bon Ton Theatre, 935 3d av

Farr Mrs. Maggie, res 841 4th av

Farrell & Chapman, insurance agents, 324 9th st

Farrell F. M. tailor, 221 9th st, bds 5th av b 9th and 10th sts

Farrell Lansing, insurance agent, res 812 4th av

Farrell Mrs. S. S. dressmaker, 808 alley

Farris Alonzo, moulder, 1726 College av

Farris Sheridan, wheel moulder, 2421 1st av

Farris Rufus, wheel moulder, 2421 1st av

Farrow Rachel, 6 w Buffington Row

Faverty James, machine agent, 3d av b 10th and 11th sts, bds 1015 6th av

Fawcett Anna, 723 2d av

Fawcett H. J. carpenter, 723 2d av

Feaknee George, machinist, bds 1829 3d av

Feeley J. T. car builder, res 1841 3d av

Feffens C. B. car builder, res 1142 3d av

FENNER WILLIAM, photographer, 403 9th st, res 812 6th av

Fenton W. E. butcher, 412 9th st, res cor 7th av and 11th st

Ferguson Annie, res 1116 3d av alley

Ferguson Charles, brakeman C. & O. R. R. res 1937 Maple av

Ferguson Cynthia, domestic, res 740 3d av

—THE—

SAFETY DEPOSIT VAULTS

—OF THE—

First ❦ National ❦ Bank

WILL BE IN OPERATION

ABOUT MAY FIRST.

Please Call and Examine the Secure Steel Vaults

IN NEW STONE BANK BUILDING.

Boxes Rented at Reasonable Rates.

DIRECTORS AND TRUSTEES:

J. L. CALDWELL.	W. H. HAGEN.	D. W. EMMONS.
GEO. F. MILLER, Jr.	B. W. FOSTER.	J. L. THORNBURG,
L H. BURKS.	D. I. SMITH.	M. C. DIMMICK.

CAPITAL, - $100,000.00.

SURPLUS AND PROFITS, $50,000.00.

Mercantile and Individual Accounts received.
Interest Paid on Time Deposits.
Money Loaned on Approved Paper.
Correspondence Invited.

The Public are INVITED to INSPECT our NEW BANKING QUARTERS.

J. L. CALDWELL, Pres.   GEO. F. MILLER, Jr., Vice-Pres.
M. C. DIMMICK, Cashier.

Ferguson Edward, machinist, res 1937 Maple av

Ferguson John H. carpenter, res 1711 8th av

Ferguson J M. merchant tailor, 1006 3d av, res same

Ferguson Mrs. John H. res 1711 1th av

Ferguson S. T. W. machine hand, res 1909 Buffington av

Ferguson Silas, tinner, 1033 3d av, res s s 2d av b 7th and 8th sts

Fetty B. L. shipping clerk, res 1421 4th av

Fetty J. C. salesman, 907 3d av, res same

Fetty W. E. clerk, res 1125 4th av

Fetty W. E. porter, rms 4th av b 12th and 13th sts

Fielder Ella, laundress, s s 4th av nr 12th st

Fielder Florence, laundress, s s 4th av nr 12th st

Fielder Lulu, laundress, s s 4th av nr 12th st

Fielder Thomas T. moulder, res 1903 5th av

Findling Caroline, res 1411 4th av

Fields Cornelius, teamster, res 1118 3d av

Feuchtenberger C. A. baker, res 647 3d av

First Baptist Church, 832 8th av, I. V. Bryant, Pastor

FIRST NATIONAL BANK. J. L. Caldwell, President. M. C. Dimmick, Cashier, 3d av

Fischback Julius, clerk, res 5th av b 9th and 10th sts

Fischer G. C. meat market, 705 9th st, res 7th av b 9th and 10th sts

Fisher B. F. machinist, res, 6 Brick Row

Fisher Frank, wks Ensign Co. res 1803 4th av

Fisher Isaac, res 1903 4th av

Fisher J. L. saloon keeper, 319 w 9th st, res same

Fisher Katie A. res 1903 4th av

Fisher Mary, domestic, res 1011 4th av

Fisher N. A. car builder, res 1901 4th av

Fisher William, wks C. & O. shops, bds 1218 4th av

Fitch Minerva, domestic, res cor 9th st and 2d av

Fitz George, plasterer, res alley b 11th and 12th sts n of 3d av

Fitz Malinda, washing, res alley b 11th and 11th sts n of 3d av

Foley H. G. dry goods merchant, 1109 3d av, res 1322 4th av

Fitzgerald Frank W. machinist, res 1916 8th av

Fitzgerald Thomas, time keeper C. & O. shops, res 1910 8th av

Fitzgerald J. H President Fitzgerald Patent Prepared Plaster Co. 324 9th st
FITZGERALD PATENT PREPARED PLAS-TER CO. J. H. Fitzgerald, President; C. D. Emmons, Vice President; W. E. Parsons, Secretary and Treasurer, office 324 9th st
Five Cent Store, P. Baer, proprietor, dealer in notions, novelties, &c. 1041 and 1043 3d av
Flanagan W. H. machinist, bds 641 5th av
Flannagan J. C. conductor C. & O. R. R. res 1344 6th av
Fletcher ——, car builder, bds 947 4th av
Fletcher Earles, moulder, res 1721 3d av
Fletcher Nellie, res 10 Beardsley Row
Fletcher John, res 10 Beardsley Row
Fliggins Ella, washing, res 1046 3d av alley
Fliggins Richard, cook Merchant's Hotel, res cor 9th st and 2d av
FLODING GEORGE A. manuf. of regalia, 1029 and 1031 3d av, res n s 6th av b 11th and 12th sts
FLORENTINE HOTEL, R. A. Mathews, prop. 9th st
Flowers Edgar W. fireman C. & O. R. R. res 917 6th av
Flowers T. W. carpenter and millwright, 917 6th av, res same
Floyd Robert, machinist, res 1744 4th av
Floyd W. A. laborer, res 1939 Maple av alley
Floyd Buck, wks Ensign Co. res 1 n Ensign
Fogg Lacy, news agent, bds 721 3d av
Foley Blanche, res n s 4th av b 12th and 13th sts
Foley Mary, res 1322 4th av
Fountain Ella, res 1674 8th av
Fountain Mrs. Stella M. res cor 1st av and 29th st
Fountain William, fireman, res 1674 8th av
Forbush E. H. drayman, res s s 5th av b 5th and 6th sts
Forbush F. R. drayman, res s s 5th av b 5th and 6th sts
Forbush J. H. drayman, s s 5th av b 5th and 6th sts
Fortier J. Quincy, bartender, res 941 3d av
Fortney Wm. moulder, res 2405 2d av
FOSTER B. W. wholesale hardware and Central Land Co's agent, 855 3d av, res 6th av
Foster C. E. carpenter, res 1739 4th av
Foster J. E. carpenter, res 1739 4th av
Foster J. W. carpenter, res 1739 4th av

Foster Jas. M. machinist, res 824 4th av
Foster Nellie, res 824 4th av
Foster R. J. brick mason, res s s 3d av, West Huntington
Foster Wm. R. res 1739 4th av
Foust A. R. car builder, bds 101 24th st
Fout Allie, servant, res 1632 2d av
Fout William, laborer, res 216 12th st
Fouty Commodore, carpenter and builder, s s 3d av w
    Huntington
Fowler Wm. traveling salesman, res 833 7th av
Fox Mrs. Catharine A. res 1522 3d av
Fox Clio D. car builder, res 1114 7th av
Fox H. B. engineer, res 1114 7th av
Fox Joe, apprentice barber, 308 4th st,
Fox Michael, res 2341 8th av
Frampton D. W. merchant, cor 3d av and 8th st, res 816
    5th av
Frampton Geo. W. (Boxley & Frampton) dealer in har-
    ness and saddles, 325 9th st, bds 1003 5th av

Frampton J. T. (Hoyt & Co.) manuf of mineral water, 745 2d av, bds Merchants Hotel
France Ada, res 1904 7th av
France J. H. laborer, res 8th st b 2d and 3d avs
France Wm. A. stone mason, res 1904 7th av
Frazier Alfred, laborer, res 1740 4th av
Frazier Ida, res 1740 4th av
Freeland Edwin, machinist, res 824 4th av
Freeman G. L. carpenter, res 812 4th av
Freeman Lucy, laundress. res 812 4th av
Freeman Rebecca, res 812 4th av
Freeman Mrs. R. V. 1005 6th av
Freeman Sallie, res 731 alley b 7th and 8th sts and 4th and 5th avs
Freeman Mrs. Sarah, res 812 4th av
Freeman Wm. res s s 3d av West Huntington
Friedman G. merchant, 928 3d av
Friedman G. (Biern & Friedman), merchant, 928 3d av, bds 848 4th av

Friend Alfred, collector Daily Herald, res 1226 3d av
Frith W. M. painter, res 1107 6th av
Froideveaux T. D. machine hand, bds 1810 4th av
Fry Livona A. 813 2d av
Fry Zillah C. res 813 2d av
Fry D. J. salesman, res 813 2d av
Fry Etta, 813 2d av
Fry John P. carpenter, res 813 2d av
Fry Kate, domestic, res 2d av b 8th and 9th sts
Fuller Ernest, res 1218 4th av
FULLER F. D. coal merchant, cor 2d av and 10th st, res 1231 4th av
Fuller Mrs. Mary E. res 1535 3d av
Fuller M. L. machinist, res 1849 3d av
Fuller Ona, res 1218 4th av
Fuller Mrs. R. M. boarding house, res 1218 4th av
Fullerton E. E. book keeper, res av b 7th and 8th sts
Fullerton E. P. clerk, res 741 3d av

G

Gaddis H. E. telegraph operator. res 317 9th st
Gaddis Mrs. H. E. boarding house, 317 9th st, res same
Galbreath Mrs. Sarah, res 1215 3d av
Gallagher Effie F. school teacher, res s s 4th av, West Huntington
Gallagher Maggie, milliner, 914 3d av, res 6th av b 8th and 9th sts
Gallagher James R. gang boss Ensign Manuf Co., res s s 4th av, West Huntington
Gallagher John, laborer, res 2213 3d av
Gallagher John, res 829 6th av
Gallagher Katie, res 829 6th av
Gallagher Maggie, clerk, res 829 6th av
Gallick Mrs. Ella, clerk, res 919 3d av
GALLICK JOSEPH, book seller and stationer, 921 3d av, res 919 3d av
Galliher J P. shiping clerk, res 1707 1th av
Galloway Henry. laborer, res 1909 4th av
Galloway Rosa. res 1909 4th av
Galloway S. T. teacher, res 1909 4th av
Galloway Wm. carpenter, res 1909 4th av
Gardner Chas. K. physician. 314 20th st. res same

JOS GALLICK,

BOOKSELLER

—AND—

STATIONER

Periodicals,

Fancy Goods,

Albums and Holiday Goods,

Gold Pens,   Blank Books,

School Supplies.

No. 921 THIRD AVENUE,

HUNTINGTON, W. VA.

B. W. FOSTER,

Wholesale and Retail Dealer in

HARDWARE, STOVES,

CUTLERY,
GUNS,

CARPENTERS' AND MACHINISTS' TOOLS,

Wagons, Buggies,

BUCKEYE MOWERS AND HARVESTERS

—AND A—

Full Line of Garden and Farm Implements.

INDUCEMENTS OFFERED CASH BUYERS.

South Side of Third Avenue,

CORNER NINTH STREET,

HUNTINGTON, W. VA.

Gardner Mrs. E. J. res 1956 4th av
Gardner Florence, col'd, 406 9th st
Gardner Thomas P. laborer, res 314 20th st
Garland Lucy, res 1303 3d av
Garland Richard H. clerk, with Simms & Enslow
Garland R. H. book keeper, 222 10th st
GARLAND THOMAS S. (Mayor of Huntington), dry goods merchant. 944 3d av, res 1251 3d av
GARLAND & VALENTINE, dry goods and notions, 946½ 3d av
Gorman Henry, drayman, res 741 2d av
Garner J. A. news agent, passenger depot
Gaskins Henry, pastry cook, 406 9th st
Gaskins James, waiter, 406 9th st
Gee Cassic, seamstress, res 1907 4th av
Geho Samuel, teamster, bds 1548 3d av
GENTRY T. F. grocer, 1121¼ 3d av, res 1055 7th av
George E. B. blacksmith, res 808 7th av
Georgia Mrs. Emma, res 613 9th st
Gerst J. V. salesman, res 1114 6th av
Gibbons Mary, student, bds 1018 6th av
Gibbs Alfred, col'd. res 830 8th av
Gibbs Frank, bds 737 2d av
Gibson Hon. Eustace, attorney at law, 933 3d av, res 728 4th av
Gibson E. St. P. res 728 4th av
Gibson Henry, laborer, res alley b 3d and 4th avs and 11th 12th sts
Gibson Howard S. res 728 4th av
Gibson James, teamster, res 1221 3d av alley
Gibson J. R. job printer. bds Merchants' Hotel
GIBSON JOHN T. prop Huntington Commercial 937 and 939 3d av up stairs, res 1054 3d av
Gibson Laura, res alley b 3d and 4th avs and 11th and 12th sts
Gibson Lee M. res 728 4th av
GIBSON & MICHIE, attorneys at law, Post Office Building
Gibson Mrs. M. F. bds 1016 6th av
Gibson Samuel, railroader, bds 523 10th st
GIBSON WESLEY A. editor Huntington Commercial, res 1054 3d av
Gibson William, fireman. 927 4th av
Gideon Will, clerk, res 950 4th av

Gideon David, clerk, res 950 4th av

GIDEON SAMUEL, clothier and gents' furnishing goods, 949 3d av, res 950 4th av

Gilkerson Leander (Lester & Co.) resturant, 834 3d av, res 713 3d av

Gillingham James, carpenter, res 844 4th av

Gillingham Mrs. James. res 844 4th av

Gillingham Mary, res 844 4th av

Gillespie George W. wks C. & O. R. R. res 1824 8th av

Gillespie G. W. Jr., machinist, res 1824 8th av

Gillespie Henry C. res 1824 8th av

Gillespie J R. carpenter, res 1854 5th av

Gillespie W. E. machinist, res 1824 8th av

Gilmore T. J. clerk, bds, 804 4th av

Gilmore M. L. car builder, res cor 5th av and 17th st

Gilmore Owen. wks C. & O. shops

Gilpin William, mail carrier, bds 753 2d av

Gipson Frank, blacksmith, res River b 25th and 26th sts

Gipson Mrs. Lavenia, bds 1231 3d av alley

Gladstone W. S. painter, res 1115 6th av

Glendening William D. machinist, res 1738 8th av

Glover Clara, col'd, res 7 Beardsley Row

Glover John, col'd, barber, 838 3d av, res 7 Beardsley Row

Glover Sumner, col'd, grocer, 3d av b 11th and 12th sts. res 7 Beardsley Row

Goard J. W. machinist, res 412 19th st

Gohen James, boss painter. res 1001 7th av

Gohen Charles, clerk, res 1001 7th av

Good Henry, col'd, plasterer, res 8 Buffington Row

Goodall Eli, car inspector, res 2d av b 4th and 5th sts

Gooderham Missouri, res 418 17th st

Gooderham William T. wks Ensign Co. res 418 17th st

Goodman Anna, res 1038 4th av

Goodman Anna, clerk, res 3d av b 7th and 8th sts

Goublin W. R. second engineer, 1016 3d av, res 3d av b 22d and 23d sts

GOODWIN & POINDEXTER, (R. A. G. & W. W. P.) prop. Carrolton Hotel, opposite C. & O. depot

Goodwin R. A. (G. & Poindexter,) prop. Carrolton Hotel, opposite C. & O. depot

Gordon A. L. carpenter, res 2129 3d av

Gordon Edward A. machinist, res 1903 4th av

44   HUNTINGTON [GRI] DIRECTORY.

Gordon H. sup't planing mill, river b 46th 17th sts, res
    1542 2d av
Gordon H. C. foreman Gordon's saw mill, res 1444 3d av
Gordon E. C. lumber inspector, res 1542 2d av
Gordon Marabell, res 1542 2d av
Gothard Benjamin, wks Gordon's mill, res 2225 3d av
Gothard C. W. carpenter, bds 1916 Maple av
Gothard J. P. wks C. & O. shops, res 25 Buffington Row
Gothard John A. blacksmith, 34 Buffington Row
Gotshall W. R. foreman Ensign foundry, res 1538 and
    1540 3d av
Gough J. B. carpenter, s s 3d av, West Huntington
Gough Lulu, coffee and spice packer, res 3d av, West
    Huntington
Gough Lulu D. clerk, res s s 3d av, West Huntington
Gould A. B. engineer C. & O. R. R. res 1805 8th av
Gouldin James, res 2213 3d av
Gouldin Warren, engineer, 2213 3d av
Goulding Mrs. B. W. dressmaker, res 742 4th av
Goulding Miss C. N. res 742 4th av
Graham J. N. sawyer, res 747 2d av
Graham Thomas, res 807 9th av
Gramm Fred, blacksmith, res 1803 4th av
Grass Crochia, res 1731 4th av
Grass J. F. car builder, res 1731 4th av
Grass Linnie, res 1731 4th av
Graves F. J. foreman C. & O. shops, res 1956 Locust av
Gray Kate, res 2121 3d av
Gray S. B. foreman Ensign Co. res 2121 3d av
Green Ella, col'd domestic, res 1021 5th av
Green John O. steward, res, 406 9th st
Green Marmaduke, railroader, res, 1401 8th av alley
Green V. M. res 1401 8th av ailey
Green W. M. col'd plastering contractor, res 814 9th av
Greenlief Allice, res 2 Buffington Row
Greenlief Allen, butcher, res 2 Buffington Row
Greenlief Amanda, res 2 Buffington Row
Greenwell H. C. merchant, 635 3d av, res same
Gregory E. M. res 937 alley
Griffin Lathan, blacksmith, res 1725 8th av
Griffin Mary, res 1725 8th av
Griffin Sidney, blacksmith, res 1725 8th av
Griffith Mary, bds 12 Brick Row
Grimes Abe, wks C. & O. shops, res 1939 Maple av

HUNTINGTON [HAG] DIRECTORY. 45

Grimes Robert A. blacksmith, 1921 Maple av
Griswold E. M. stone mason, 1346 3d av
Grooms C. D. saloon keeper, 3d av b 8th and 9th sts, res
    4th av b 7th and 8th sts
Grooms H. W. bar tender, res 715 4th av
Groves Lake, porter, res 941 3d av
Gue Samuel, wks Ensign Co. res 1740 College av
Guinn C. H. & Bro. grocers, 1928 8th av, res same
Gunn W. J. clerk, bds 1018 6th av
Gwinn Bros. (O. E. G. & W. W. G.) prop. Aldine Roller
    Mills, 954 2d av
Gwinn C. E. traveling salesman, res 1312 3d av
Gwinn C. H. boiler maker, res 1926 8th av
Gwinn Effie. res 1926 8th av
Gwinn O. W. carpenter, res 1926 8th av
Gwinn O. E. manager Aldine Roller Mills, bds e s 4th av
    nr 10th st
Gwinn W. W. (G. Bros.) res 410 10th st
Gwinn W. W. book-keeper, res e s 4th av nr 10th st

H

Hackworth Edward, flagman, res 802 7th av
Hackworth George, res 802 7th av
Haeberle Jacob. carpenter, res 1917 5th av
Haeberle John, moulder, res 420 19th st
Hafner C. L. Sr. President Belt Line Street R. R. Co.
Hafner Louise, res 1334 3d av
Hagan Bernard, engineer, res 1019 7th av
HAGAN & BRO. (J. B. H. & R. E. H.) dealers in
    hardware, tinware and slate, 1033 3d av
Hagan Chris. clerk, res 1005 6th av
Hagan R. E. (H. & Bro.) dealers in hardware, 1033 3d av,
    res n s 6th av b 10 and 11th sts
Hagen H. B. (Royal Coffee and Spice Co.) wholesale gro-
    cer. 1016 3d av
Hagen Joseph. (H. & Bro.) dealer in hardware, 1033 3d
    av, res 1030 7th av
Hagen James W. res 1312 4th
Hagen Hon. W. H. banker, First National Bank, res cor
    1st av and 29th st
Hager George D. blacksmith. res 2001 8th av
Hague C. W. car builder, res 1911 3d av

Hague Cora C. res 1911 3d av
Hague Sarah E. res 1911 3d av
Hague V. D. canvasser, res 1911 3d av
Hague W. H. blacksmith, res 1911 3d av
Haig Rosco V. teamster, res 1215 3d av
Haley Charles B. wks C. & O. shops, res 818 7th av
Haley Tolbert, res 820 7th av
Hall A. E. carpenter, res 649 3d av
Hall D. R. locomotive engineer, res 1007 6th av
Hall Emma, res 1335 3d av
Hall George F. tinner, res 1 Frame Row
Hall J. R. carpenter, res 2 Frame Row
Hall James, machine hand, res 1905 5th av
Hall James S. core maker, 1917 3d av
Hall S. R. oil dealer, res 649 3d av
Hall Susan, dress maker, 324 9th st, res 730 3d av
Hall T. J. conductor, res 1225 6th av
Hall Trevor, car builder, 1046 4th av
Hallanan Mrs. Mattie, res 524 e 8th st
Hallanan Dr. Thomas, (H. & Davis), physician and sur-
    823 3d av,
Halley Mertic, res 14th st b 2d and 3d avs
Halley John S. laborer, res 2d av b 8th and 9th sts
Halstead I. B. fireman, res 809 7th av
Halstead Miss Ottie, res 809 7th av
HOLSWADE W. H. H. furniture, carpets and un-
    dertaking, 943 and 945 3d av, res 947 3d av
Ham R. A. apprentice, bds 1231 5th av
Hambleton Edward, carpenter, 1116 4th av
HAMBLETON M. N. monumental works, 215 9th st,
    res 1213 6th av
Hambleton Wilber, marble works, 215 9th st, res 1210 3d
    av
Hamblin S. R. carpenter, res 8 Frame Row
Haney Homer, plasterer, bds 721 2d av
Hamilton Anna, res 1105 3d av alley
Hamilton J. engineer, bds 916 5th av
Hamilton J. Q. carpenter, res 1812 5th av
Hamilton K. L. clerk, res 909½ 7th av
Hamilton Otto J. res 1812 4th av
Hamilton Robert, lineman, res 1105 3d av alley
Hamlin Charles, teamster, 725 alley b 7th and 8th sts and
    4th and 5th avs
Hamlin Fred A. butcher, res 310 21st st

Hamlin Miss H. res 725 alley b 7th and 8th sts and 4th and 5th avs
Hamlin Mac, wheel cleaner, bds 314 21st st
Hamlin J. A. teamster, bds cor 8th st and 2d av
Hamlin Minnie, res 310 21st st
Hamlin William, wheel cleaner, res 310 21st st
Hamlin Thomas, blacksmith, res 725 alley b 7th and 8th sts and 4th and 5th avs
Hamlin Thomas, machine hand, 8 Buffington Row
Hamlin William, laborer, bds cor 8th st and 2d av
Hampton C. W. engineer, res 1709 4th av
Hampton James, laborer, bds 1942 8th av
Hancock Adam, wagon maker, res 2d av b 4th and 5th sts
Handley Gertrude, res 743 alley b 7th and 8th sts and 4th and 5th avs
Handley George, machinist, res 8th st b 4th and 5th avs
Handley J. W. laborer, res 733 alley b 7th and 8th sts and 4th and 5th avs
Handley Kate, res 733 alley b 7th and 8th sts and 4th and 5th avs
Handlin Charles Leslie, clerk, res 1115 4th av
Handlin Mrs. Mattie B. dress maker, res 1115 4th av
Handlin Nookie, res 1115 4th av
Hanlin Robert T. carpenter, res 1115 4th av
Haney Mrs. Robert F. res 1044 3d av
Hankins William, col'd, porter, rms 901 6th av
Hanley L. M. capitalist, 1003 5th av, res same
Hanley Pearl, res 1003 5th av
Hanley Harry L. res 1003 5th av
Hann C. M. shipping clerk, rms cor 3d av and 10th st
Hanna Edward E. cooper, res 1526 3d av
Hanna J. M. cooper, res 1526 3d av
Hanna Jefferson D. engineer, res 942 7th av
Harber W. O. brakeman, res 1413 R. R.
Hardbarger M. C. brakeman, 1714 8th av rear
Harbour James, res 1730 5th av
HARDING B. B. prop.Anchor Bottling Wks, 947 2d av
Hardy Commodore, col'd. porter, res 831 7th av alley
Hardy Mobile, waiter, 406 9th st
Harmon Charles, butcher, 749 and 751 3d av, res n s 3d av nr 7th st
Harmon Clinton, carpenter, res 6 n Ensign Shops

C. HAUCKE & SONS,

—DEALERS IN—

WALL PAPER!

—AND—

WALL PAPER HANGINGS!

—A LARGE STOCK OF—

WALL PAPER AND MOULDINGS

CONSTANTLY KEPT ON HAND.

PAPER HANGING DONE IN THE VERY
BEST STYLE.

LEE HAUCKE,

House, Sign and Decorative Painting.

SIGN WORK A SPECIALTY.

No. 954 THIRD AVENUE,

HUNTINGTON, W. VA.

Harmon Monroe, sewing machine agent, bds 1941 Buffington av

• Harris A. L. carpenter, res West Huntington

Harris C. A. painter, res 1905 5th av

Harris Eddie, musician, bds Merchants' Hotel

Harris Eli, col'd, waiter, res 801 2d av

Harris J. B. clerk, res 529 12th st

Harris Mary, col'd, domestic, res 406 9th st

Harris Mrs. Myrtle, actress Bon Ton, bds Merchants' Hotel

Harris Olie, col'd, domestic, res alley b 11th and 12th st a :d 2d and 3d avs

Harrison Charles, laborer, bds 4 Frame Row

Harrison Charles, contractor, res 1955 Virginia av

Harrison Dinnie, res 1117 3d av

Harrison Flora, school teacher, res 1955 Virginia av

Harrison J. H. policeman, 37 Buffington Row

Harrison Mary, school teacher, res 1955 Virginia av

Harrison Nellie, res 1955 Virginia av

Harrison Otis, 1955 Virginia av

Harrison Sinia, res 37 Buffington Row

Harrison W. R. blacksmith, 1752 4th av

Harrold C. B. (H. & Miller,) insurance and real estate agent, 920 3d av, res 1032 4th av

Harrold George W. blacksmith, res 2020 4th av

Harrold Ira O. blacksmith, res 2020 4th av

Harrold J. M. res 2020 4th av

Harrold J. M. Jr. apprentice moulder, res 2020 4th av

Harrold & Miller, insurance and real estate agents, 920 3d av

Hartley William, clerk, res 1946 7th av

Hartman Anna M. 1338 3d av

Hartman Edward, clerk, res 529 12th st

Hartman F. M. attorney at law and stenographer, 222 10th st, rms same

Hartman Rosa, res 647 3d av

Harvey H. C. (Royal Coffee and Spice Co,) wholesale grocer, 1016 3d av, res s s 3d av b 13th and 14th sts

Harvey Col. Robert T. capitalist, 1006 6th av, res same

• Harvey Hon. Thomas H. Circuit Judge, 8th Judicial District W. Va. res West Huntington

HARVEY, HAGEN & CO. (H. C. H., H. B. H. & G. F. Miller, Jr.) wholesale grocers, 907 3d av

Harwood C. B. painter, res 1434 3d av

Haskell N. D. machinist, res 1807 8th av
Haskell Homer E. fireman, rms 947 4th av
Haskin Mary, domestic, 406 9th st
Haskin Lulu, domestic, 1304 3d av
Hastings A. C. carpenter, res 1035 7th av
Hastings John, carpenter, res 913 4th av
Hatch Charles, engineer, res 529 12th st
Hatcher W. H. machinist, res 19 Frame Row
Hatfield Thomas, clerk, res 1214 4th av
Haucke Albert S. painter, s s 7th av b 9th and 10th sts
Haucke Conrad, paper hanger, res s s 7th av b 9th and 10th sts
Haucke Fred L. painter, res 914 7th av
Haucke Lee, sign painter, res 914 7th av
HAUCKE & SONS, wall paper and paper hanging, 953 3d av res 914 7th av
Haucke Theresa, res 419 7th av
Hawes A. W. car inspector, res 1698½ 8th av
Hawkins J. L. (Emmons & Marr), 902 3d av
Hawkins Charles M. postal clerk, res 1232 3d av
Hawkins L. G. plumber, 324 9th st, res 1232 3d av
Hawkins Thomas, Jr. engineer, 918 7th av
Haworth Allie, music teacher, res 632 10th st
Haworth Essie, res 632 10th st
Haworth Dr. E. C. physician and surgeon, res 632 10th st
Haworth Mrs. Hannah, res 632 10th st
Haworth Lella, teacher, Madison, Ind. res 632 10th st
Hay Addie, res 1137 3d av
Hay C. C. car builder, res 1837 3d av
Hay Mary B. res 1837 3d av
Hay Sophia, res 1837 3d av
Hay Strother, teamster, res 1837 3d av
Hay Strother Jr. car builder, res 1837 3d av
Hays Ella, res 817 4th av
Hays Mrs. Eunice, res 817 4th av
Hays Florence, res n 24th st
Hays Georgia, res 817 4th av
Hearholger William, moulder, res 312 19th st
Heartley F. C. car builder, res 1950 Buffington av
Heartly George, bds 1950 Buffington av
Heath Lucinda, col'd, res 817 6th av
Hecox E. C. (H. & Williams.) attorney, 324 9th st, res 6th av b 7th and 8th sts

P. HENSON,

 **STONE**  **MASON**

Contracts for All Kinds of Stone
Work taken at

THE MOST REASONABLE RATES.

ALL WORK WARRANTED.

*Headquarters at the Office of Millender &
Bierman,*

No. 1113 Third Avenue,

HUNTINGTON, W. VA.

HECOX & WILLIAMS, (E. C. H. & E. E. W.) attorneys, 324 9th st

Heck David, baggage master, res 615 10th st

Hendrick Andrew, res 4 Beardsley Row

Hendrick Ella, res 4 Beardsley Row

Hendrick Henry, laborer, res 1803 4th av

Heffner J. F. cupola tender, res 1911 Maple av

Heller P. P. machinist, res s s 5th av b 5th and 6th sts

Helms Fannie, res 1836 4th av

Helstern Joseph, prop. Gem Saloon, 3d av b 9th and 10th sts, res 1018 4th av

Henderson Mamie, clerk, res 7th av b 9th and 10th sts

Henderson T. E. surveyor, res 913 7th av

Henkle George, grocer, 1946 7th av, res same

Hennings Dr. George, physician, 317 9th st, res same

Hennion J. H sup't Ensign Co. res 1701 3d av

Henley C. R. carpenter, res 1729 8th av

Henley M. V. res 1729 8th av

Henry Frank, blacksmith, bds 101 24th st

Henry James, saw filer, bds 1245 3d av

Henry John, carpenter, res 825 7th av

Henry Mrs. Mary, res 819 6th av

Hensley Ella, res 910 7th av

Hensley Solomon, laborer, res 316 21st st

Hensley William, machine hand, 1938 7th av

Hensley William E. wks Ensign Co. res 316 21st st

Hensen Erastus, laborer, res 1936 6th av

HENSON P. stone mason and contractor, 1113 3d av

Herbert Ack, tailor, 905 3d av, bds e s 8th st b 4th and 5th avs

Herbert Mrs. Laura, res 823 3d av

Herbert Lou, baker, 823 3d av, res same

Herman G. machinist, res 529 12th st

Herndon Mrs. Effie May, res 1015 6th av

Herndon John W. clerk, res 1015 6th av

Hern Harvey, teamster, res 1955 Virginia av

HERRING W. W. prop. St. Charles Hotel, 901 6th av, res same

Herring Maggie A. res 901 6th av

Herring Mary E. res 901 6th av

Herz Philip, clerk, res 950 4th av

Hess William, tinner, res, 824 4th av

Hessburg Clara, res 1020 7th av

Hester William, railroader, res 621 11th av

Hetter H. E. blacksmith, 1856 4th av
Hicks Charley, laborer; res s s 3d av, West Huntington
Hicks Marietta, res 835 3d av
Higgins A. L. supt. 927 2d av, res 6th av b 11th and 12th sts
Higgins C. G. insurance, 324½ 9th st, res 1214 4th av
Higgins Edward, moulder, bds 101 24th st
Higgins Ellenorah, res 1133 6th av
Higgins George, laborer, res 1803 4th av
Higgins J. P. carpenter, res 1803 4th av
Higgins James, bds 101 24th st
Higgins Thomas, carpenter, res 1848 8th av
Higginson J. C. wks C. & O. R. R. res 705 9th st
Higginson M. W. car inspector, res 1684 8th av
Higginson Maggie, res 1684 8th av
Hill A. B. contractor, res 743 4th av
Hill Miss C. E. res 743 4th av
Hill C. W. carpenter, res 1119 3d av
HILL DANDRIDGE, grocery and resturant, 713 9th st
Hill G. W. carpenter, res 743 4th av
Hill L. S. wks C. & O. shops, res 743 4th av
HILTON GLENN, optician and jeweler, 321 9th st, res 4th av b 9th and 10th sts
Hineman B. E. carpenter, res 1529 3d av
Hinerman David, machinist, res 2 Brick Row
Hinerman Oscar, res 2 Brick Row
Hinerman Walker, engineer, res 2 Brick Row
Hinerman Walter, engineer, res 2 Brick Row
Hinerman William, machinist, res 2 Brick Row
Hines M. blacksmith, bds 1829 3d av
Hiter Hugh, col'd, laborer, res 1529 3d av

Hiter John, col'd, porter, res 836 6th av

Hitt Jennie, res 1941 4th av

Hoback Mrs. Adah, res 721 3d av

Hoback Mrs Annie, col'd, res 832 3d av

Hoback Flora, res 721 3d av

Hoback Frank, fireman, res 7 Brick Row

Hoback Fred. printer, res 721 3d av

Hoback Gertrude, res 721 3d av

Hoback Mae, res 721 3d av

Hobson Plummer, machinist, res 529 12th st

HODGES THOMAS E. Secretary and Treasurer Advertiser Publishing Co. and Principal Marshall College, the State Normal School, res Marshall College

Hodges Mrs. Thomas E. res Marshall College

Hoffman Beulah, 828 3d av

Hoffman Mrs. Etta, book agent, res 828 3d av

Hoffman H. H. stone mason, res 828 3d av

Hoffman John, Sr., engineer, res 511 13th st

Hoffman John Jr., 511 13th st

Hoffman W. H. res 828 3d av

HOFF FRANK, jeweler, 923 3d av

Hoge James, tailor, res 1116 4th av

Hoge Mollie, 1116 4th av

Hogg Annie, res 1632 6th av

Hogg C. L. feed merchant, 3d av b 7th and 8th sts, res 1021 5th av

Hogg Estella, school teacher, res 1632 6th av

Hogg Herbert, glazier, res 16th st b 4th and 5th avs

Hogg L. M. grocery clerk, res 636 10th st

Hogg T. F. res 1632 6th av

Hogg William N. res 1632 6th av

Hoyt Fred. (Hoyt & Co) bottler, West Huntington

Hogsett R. F. res 823 6th av

Holden Ida, domestic, res 524 11th st

Holden Mabel, res 1804 4th av

Holderby Mrs. C. A. market gardener, 16th st s of C. & O. R. R.

Holden S. M. carpenter, res 23 Buffington Row

Holderby Lucy M. res 1905 Buffington av

Holderby W. R. stone mason, res 1905 Buffington av

Holland Roy, laborer, wks Ensign Co., res n 24th st

Holley Neil, laborer, res 1924 Buffington av

Holley John, laborer, res Love Block

Holloron Katie, res 4th av nr 12th st

Holloron T. P. telegraph operator, res 4th av nr 12th st

Holloway Ella, res 309 11th st

Holly Mrs. Caroline, col'd, boarding house, 1212 4th av alley

Holmes Charles, cook, 406 9th st

Holmes Flora, res 24 Buffington Row

Holon William, col'd, laborer, res 14 west Buffington Row

Holt John H. attorney, 3d av b 8th and 9th sts, res 615 9th st

Holtzworth Jacob, butcher, 3d av b 7th and 8th sts, res 1331 4th av

HOOD E. E. editor Herald, 308 10th st, res 10th av b 12th and 13th sts

Hoover Mary, res 1526 3d av

Hope L. A. wks C. & O. office, res 605 9th st

Hopkins Albert F. cook, 941 3d av

Hopkins Bell, col'd, laundress, res 1117 4th av alley

Hopkins Miss Q. H. col'd, res s s 5th av b 4th and 5th sts

Hopkins Richard, col'd, laborer, res s s 5th av b 4th and 5th sts

Hopkins Thomas, col'd, teamster, res s s 5th av b 4th and 5th sts

Hopewell Lucy, col'd, res 4 west Buffington Row

Horn Annie, res 3 Brick Row

Horn Benjamin, carpenter, res 3 Frame Row

Horn Ida M. res 3 Frame Row

Horn Mamie W. res 3 Frame Row

Howard A. W. tool dresser, res 1917 Virginia av

Howard Frank, car painter, res 1107 6th av

Howell A. C. brick contractor, bds 1318 4th av

Howell Emma, res 1318 4th av

Howelle P. L. painter, res 317 10th st

Hoyt J. A. (Huntington Bottling Works), manuf of mineral waters, 745 2d av, res West Huntington

Hubbard Ack, tailor, bds 416 8th st

Hudson Emma B. res 1901 8th av

Hudson H. H. plumber, res 711 6th av

Hudson Laura L. res 1901 8th av

Hudson Morris, blacksmith, res 1945 8th av

Hudson Peter, laborer, res 1901 8th av

Hudson W. H. laborer, res 1901 8th av

Huff David, laborer, res 1817 Virginia av

Huff Frank, teamster, bds w s 11th st b 4th and 5th avs

HUFF H. LINN, coal dealer, res 729 6th av

OFFICE OF

Huntington Bed Lounge Comp'y.

HUNTINGTON, WEST VA., MARCH 19, 1891.

DEAR SIR:—

We beg leave to call your attention to our new enterprise, i. e.: the manufacture of Bed Lounges exclusively for the trade. We are now fully prepared with a large stock of Lounge Frames and a well assorted stock of

Tapestry, Body Brussels, and Velvet Carpets, Moquettes, Silks and Plushes, and Patterns

in all their varieties to fill orders as fast as received. We finish our Frames in Walnut, Oak, Antique Oak, 16th Century and Old English Oak, as ordered, and will upholster in any color or style desired, on short notice. Our workmen are first-class in their several departments, and have strict instructions to do good work only. Our prices are very low on each lounge, as we expect our profit to come from the large number we manufacture and sell. Soliciting a trial order from you, we believe it will be the means of making you a regular customer. Hoping to hear from you soon, we are,

Respectfully yours,

HUNTINGTON LOUNGE CO

A. B. PALMER, Sec'y & Treas.

Huff J. A. blacksmith, res 1142 3d av
Huff J. M. carpenter, res 1328 4th av
Hughes Bertram, res 1932 4th av
Hughes David, blacksmith, res 1932 4th av
Hughes Fred. laborer, bds 101 24th st
Hughes Samuel, laborer, res 3 n Ensign
Hughes Thomas, machine hand, res 2 Burks Row
Hughes William, res 1932 4th av
Hulbert Charles J. carpenter, res 1832 8th av
Hulbert Dorah, res 1832 8th st
Hull A. J. time keeper, res 1007 6th av
Humphrey Colonel, carpenter, res 1017 7th av
Humphrey L. W. (Matthews & H.) photographer, bds 6th
    av b 7th and 8th sts
Humphry Robert, col'd, laborer, res 994 8th av
Hundley E. W. wood machinist, res 1917 3d av
Hungerford Grace, res 818 6th av

Hungerford M. C. carpenter, 818 6th av
Hunnicutt Lizzie, 1018 6th av
Hunt G. W. col'd. barber, res 38 Buffington Row
Hunt Henry. col'd. laborer, res 3 Buffington Row
Hunt Mrs. Polly, res 1124 6th av
Hunter C. W. agent C. & O. freight depot
Huntington, Bank of, general bankers, (John H. Russell,
President. F. B. Enslow. Vice Pres. James K. Oney,
Cashier. Organized 1872. Capital stock, $50.000.00),
1002 3d av
Huntington & Big Sandy R. R. Co., J. L. Caldwell, Secre-
tary and Treasurer, over First National Bank
HUNTINGTON DAILY ADVERTISER CO. 835
3d av
Huntington Electric Light and Street Railroad Co., J.
L. Caldwell, President. office over First Nat. Bank
HUNTINGTON GAZETTE, George R. McIntosh,
prop. 835 3d av
HUNTINGTON HOTEL, G. W. Hutchinson, prop.
753 and 755 2d av
Huntington Ice and Storage Co., 904 2d av
**HUNTINGTON & KENOVA LAND DEVEL-
OPMENT CO.,** J. L. Caldwell, Treasurer and Gen-
eral Manager, over First Nat. Bank
HUNTINGTON LOUNGE CO. George F. Miller,
Pres. A. B. Palmer, Secy and Treas. (George F. Mil-
ler, A. B. Palmer, John L. Johnston and Johnston
and Emmons). 723 3d av
Huntington Post Office, H. M. Adams, Post Master, cor
4th av and 9th st, res 1047 4th av
**HUNTINGTON PRINTING & PUBLISHING
CO.,** publishers Huntington Daily Herald, 308 10th
st. Organized Dec. 18, 1890. Capital stock, $5,000. E.
M. Campbell, President. E. E. Hood, Secretary and
General Manager. J. F. Ellis. Treasurer
HUTCHINSON G. W. prop. Huntington Hotel, 753
and 755 2d av
HUTCHINSON LON H. manager Western Union
Telegraph Office. 216 10th st, res 216½ 10th st
HUNTINGTON WATER CO. D. W. Immel, mana-
ger. 913½ 3d av, res 607 9th st
Hutchinson Mrs. Lon H. telegraph operator, res 216½ 10th
st

Hutchinson Mrs. T. 753 and 755 cor 8th and 2d av
Hutchinson Will, clerk, res cor 2d av and 8th st
Hyatt George, res 1131 6th av

I

IMMEL D. W. superintendent Water Works, 913 3d
av, res 607 9th st
Ingram George, machinist, cor 2d av and 10th st, res 911
6th av
INGRAM & O'NEILL, (Geo. I. & Thos. O'N.), Ma-
chine Shop and Foundry, 949 2d av
Innis E. J. res 1020 7th av
Innis Martha, res 1020 7th av
Innis Nettie, res 1020 7th av
Irvin W. L. chief clerk at C. & O. freight depot, rms 918
4th av
Isbell Mrs. C. A. res 1019 6th av
Isbell Irving J. res 1019 6th av
Isbell Lillian, res 1019 6th av
ISBELL L. D. attorney at law, 916 3d av, res 1019 9th
av

J

JACK R. A. (J. & Co.) merchant, 940 3d av, res 3d av
nr 13th st
Jackson Henry, carpenter, res 7 Brick Row
Jackson A. L. engineer, res 1730 8th st
Jackson Dora, col'd res 1680 8th av
Jackson J. T. col'd, school janitor, res 417 9th st
Jackson Morgan, col'd, res 2d av b 8th and 9th sts
Jackson Morris, col'd, porter, res 816 8th av
Jackson William, col'd, wks Gordon's saw mill, res 1680
8th av
Jacobs H. tailor, 905 3d av, res cor 3d av and 7th st
Jacoby Boyd, painter, bds 926 6th av
Jackson James, teamster, res 1955 Virginia av
James Susie, col'd, res 1680 8th av
JAMES W. O. col'd, contractor and street paver, res
813 8th st
Javin William H. fireman, bds 808 4th av
Jarvis Emma A. res cor 3d av and 14th st

WILLIAM O. JAMES,

STREET PAVER

—AND—

CONTRACTOR.

Is prepared with his own teams to do EXCAVATING
and FILLING on short notice and at reasonable rates.
All work done in good style and

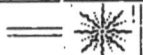 Fully Warranted.

He is not a novice, nor a new-comer, but is one of the
first settlers, and his work in various parts of the city
shows for itself.   His motto is

HONEST WORK.

REASONABLE CHARGES.

PERFECT SATISFACTION

Residence, 813 Eighth St.

HUNTINGTON, W. VA.

✳✳✳✳ *Reasons* ✳✳✳✳

WHY WE WE ARE ALWAYS BUSY!

WE OFFER YOU A LARGE AND SPLENDID ASSORTMENT OF

Dry Goods and Notions

We challenge comparison from any quarter for magnitude, variety and general excellence of assortment. Our prices are always found to be the lowest, and our goods of the best quality and of the most fashionable designs. We sell low price goods as well as the finest grades in foreign and domestic makes. Our clerks are always polite and willing to show goods, and endeavor to please you, and make you feel at home in our store. We invite every body to call and inspect our stock, and compare prices, and see who does the best for you.

R. A. JACK & CO.

No. 940 Third Ave.

Jarvis George, S. (J. & Bros.) machinist, 202 10th st, res cor 3d av and 14th st
Jarvis Ida B. res cor 3d av and 14th st
Jarvis John, laborer, res 5th av b 19th and 20th sts
Jarvis J. C. (J. & Bros.) machinist. res 907 6th av
JARVIS & BROS. (G. S. J., W. F. J., J. H. J., & J. C. J.) machinists, 202 10th st
Jarvis John H. (J. & Bros.) 202 10th st, res 613 10th st
Jarvis Sarah E. res 3d av and 14th st
Jarvis William. painter, res 1912 4th av
Jarvis Walter F. (J. & Bros.) machinist, 202 10th st, res cor 3d av and 14th st
Jasper J. M. col'd, drayman, res 613 3d av
Jasper Matilda, col'd, res 613 3d av
Jeffers E. F. laborer, res 26 Buffington Row
Jeffers John H. laborer, res 26 Buffington Row
Jefferson Maggie, res 18 Buffington Row

JARVIS & BRO.

MACHINISTS

. . . . .

—ALL KINDS OF—

Locomotive Tires Turned.

LOCOMOTIVE REPAIRS A SPECIALTY.

MANUFACTURERS OF

THE ✛ IMPROVED ✛ JARVIS ✛ ENGINE ✛ GOVERNOR.

HUNTINGTON, W. VA.

Jefferson Laura, res 18 Buffington Row
Jeffers Emerson H. laborer, res 26 Buffington Row
Jenkins Amanda, col'd, res 1735 8th av
Jenkins H. W. clerk, res 1713 3d av
Jenkins Lindsey, dairyman. 1037 3d av, res same
Jenkins B. W. blacksmith, res 1911 Maple av
Jenkins R. C. blacksmith, res 13 Frame Row
Jennings F. M. merchant, 2413 1st av, res same
Jenkins Miss S. res 1312 3d av
Jenkins Sophia, col'd, res 1735 8th av
Jenkins Trent, contractor, res 1735 8th av
Jennings Idella, res 2413 1st av
Jennings Joseph F. res 2413 1st av
Jewell W. H. teamster, res 1802 5th av

Jewett James H. foreman Eureka laundry, res 1118½ 4th av
Jimison Alexander, col'd, stone mason, res cor 9th av and
  14th sts
Jimison Talitha, col'd, res cor 9th av and 14th st
Jinkins Frank, porter, bds 951 3d av
Jobe William, machinist, res 643 3d av
Jobe Carlos, bill poster, res 643 3d av

62	HUNTINGTON [JOH] DIRECTORY.

Jobe Hattie, res 643 3d av
Jobe Mrs. J. R. res 642 3d av
Jobe Mary, res 643 3d av
Joice Lilly, stewardess, Florentine Hotel
Johnson Abner T. car builder, res n s 3d av, West Huntington
Johnson Alfred, col'd. wks C. & O. yards, res 1533 8th av
Johnson Alice, col'd, res 213 8th st
Johnson David, conductor, res 819 6th av
Johnson Dean, col'd, res 840 8th av
Johnson E. E. bar tender, 308 7th st
Johnson Emma, col'd, cook, res 1244 4th av
Johnson Mrs. H. S. res 216½ 10th st
Johnson John, fireman, res 1107 6th av
Johnson John, col'd, brakeman, bds 2d av b 8th and 9th
Johnson Julia, col'd, cook, res 529 12th st
Johnson L. C. brakeman, res 1044 4th av
Johnson James A. laborer, res 9 Frame Row
Johnson Lizzie, col'd, domestic, 719 alley b 2d and 3d avs and 7th and 8th sts
Johnson Mary J. res 1044 4th av
Johnson Morris, laborer, 213 8th st
Johnson M. S. general merchandise, 741 7th av, res 732 6th av
Johnson Ned, col'd, res 827 4th av
Johnson Mrs. N. J. dressmaker, res 2d av b 5th and 6th sts
Johnson P. A. carpenter, 2d av b 5th and 6th sts
Johnson Robert, col'd, peddler, 846 3d av alley
Johnson William, col'd. clerk, res 621 11th st
Johnson William, col'd, res 713 9th st
Johnston James E. furniture dealer, 1041 3d av, res 1144 6th av
Johnston Belle, domestic, res 944 4th av
Johnston Dan, col'd, 1329 3d av
Johnston Daniel, col'd, res 5 w Buffington Row
JOHNSTON & EMMONS, (J. E. J. & J. A. E.) dealers in furniture, 944 3d av
Johnston Frank E. brakeman, res s s 3d av, West Huntington
Johnston I. B. blacksmith, res 1707 4th av
Johnston H. W. merchant, s s 3d av, West Huntington, res same

Johnson Lee Long, wks brick yard, res s s 3d av, West Huntington alley
Johnston James E. (J. & Emmons,) furniture dealer, 944 3d av, res cor 6th av and 12th st
Johnston J. B. conductor, res 1023 14th st
Johnston J. S. teamster, res 1529 3d av
Johnston May, res 1342 6th av
Johnston Mary, res 5 w Buffington Row
Johnston Martha, res 1023 14th st
Johnston N. B. car builder, res s s 3d av, West Huntington
Johnston Owen W. painter, res s s 3d av West Huntington
Jolly R. L. gang boss, res 1228 4th av
Jones Mrs. Amelia, res 215 8th st
Jones Anna E. res 1104 3d av
Jones Mrs. Charlotte, washing, res 1215 3d av alley
Jones Elizabeth, res 2311 8th av
Jones C. H. wks C. & O. shops, res 215 8th st
Jones Cal J. car inspector, res 1544 3d av
Jones Mrs. Eliza, nurse, res 1215 3d av alley
Jones Levi, car builder, res 1923 Buffington av
Jones Emma, domestic, res 1956 Locust av
Jones Edward, engineer, res 1936 Locust av
Jones Grant, laborer, res 1936 Locust av
Jones L. carpenter, res 19 Buffington Row
Jones Benjamin, res 19 Buffington Row
Jones E. M. conductor, res 1104 3d av
Jones Gertie, col'd, res 827 4th av
Jones James, laborer, res 1938 Maple av
Jones John, bar keeper, bds 701 5th av
JONES JOHN A. dealer in musical instruments, 1041 3d av, res 1031 5th av
Jones Lewis, moulder, res 1902 4th av
Jones Martha S. res 943 4th av
Jones A. Oscar, Oak Hall saloon, res 1104 3d av,
Jones Mr. T. B. conductor, res 1338 11th av alley
Jones Thomas, laborer, 1215 3d av alley
Jones William, col'd, waiter, res cor 9th st and 2d av
Jones William, printer, res 1125 4th av
Jones W. E. engineer, res cor 20th st and Locust av.
Jordon C. R. carpenter, res 1918 8th av
Jordon S. res 1920 Locust av
Jordon Miss S. N. res 1920 Locust av

64   HUNTINGTON [KEL] DIRECTORY.

Jordon W. H. laborer, res 1920 Locust av
Jordon Miss F. J. res 1920 Locust av
Jordon Mrs. W. A. res 101 24th st
Jordon Edna, bds 101 24th st
Jordon J. F. carpenter, res 1920 Locust av
Justice Lizzie, washing, res 1042 3d av alley
Justice P. F. plumber, bds 711 6th av

K

Kahn Mrs. Lena, dress goods and millinery, 906 3d av, res same
Kahn Jacob, saloon keeper, 846 3d av, bds 4th av b 10th 11th sts
Kahn Lee, dry goods merchant, 906 3d av, res same
Kain Bernard, blacksmith, res 2003 8th av
Kaine Anna, res 2003 8th av
Kaine Martin, res 2003 8th av
Kale Jennie, domestic, res 726 6th av
Keathley A. O. machine hand, res 1916 Buffington av
Keathley Charles E. boiler maker, res 1916 Buffington av
Keefe J. F. yardmaster, C. & O. R. R. res 614 and 616 10th st
KEEFE WILLIAM, druggist, 934 3d av, res 824 7th av
Keenan Clay, railroader, res 623 10th st
Keenan Newton, clerk, res 623 10th st
Kenny Edward, col'd, section work, res 1 Buffington Row
Kenny Lettie, col'd, res 1 Buffington Row
Keeney Myrtle, res 2251 8th av
Keeney M. E. brakeman, res 419 8th st
Keeney Theresa, res 810 alley b 2d and 3d avs and 8th and 9th sts
Keeney W. H. laborer, res 810 alley b 2d and 3d avs and 8th and 9th sts
Keeler James, blacksmith, res 2016 4th av
Keller Jefferson D. machinist, res 1942 Buffington av
Kelley Effey A. res 1110 4th av
Kelly F. M. blacksmith, res 1427 4th av
Kelly H. H. (H. H. K. & Co.) clothing merchant, 854 3d av, bds 1309 3d av
KELLY H. H. & CO., (H. H. K. & T. S. Garland), general clothiers, 854 3th av
Kelly Oscar, clerk, res 904 3d av

J. H. KENNET.   J. H. MARCUM.

Leading Livery Stable

IN THE CITY.

CAREFUL DRIVERS Furnished When Desired.

Handsome Equipages and Fine Horses.
Fire Proof Stable. New Rigs.

FINE HEARSE

—AND—

BURIAL APPOINTMENTS!

Fine Horses, and Everything in First-
Class City Style.

If you want a fine turn-out for driving, go to the oldest and most
reliable stable in town.

KENNET & MARCUM,

714, 716, 718, 720, 722 & 724 Third Av.

OPEN DAY AND NIGHT.

Kelner Lester, liquor dealer, 1017 3d av, res same

Kenly Mrs. Nora, col'd, laundress, res 729 alley b 6th and 7th sts

Kennedy Anna, cook, res 1116 4th av

Kennett Annie, res 539 9th st

Kennett Frank, res 539 9th st

KENNETT & MARCUM, livery and sale stable, 704 3d av

Kennett John, (J. K. & Marcum), livery and sale stable 714 and 716 3d av, res 725 and 727 3d av

Kennett Letitia F. res 725 3d av

Kennett Levi, res 725 and 727 3d av

Kennett William, res 539 9th st

Kent C. H. engineer, res 931½ 3d av

Kent James, teamster, res 3d av

Kent R. E. machinist, res 1747 4th av

Kerby Jennie, servant, res 1054 3d av

Kerr Jessie, res 830 7th av

Kerr Len. molder, res 1 Burks Row

Kerlin John W. carpenter, bds 1 Brick Row

Ketchen George, laborer, res 215 alley

Ketner C. W. boiler maker, res 1136 7th av

Ketner Edward, res 1136 7th av

Ketner Flora, res 1136 7th av

Keys Charles, barber, 929 3d av, res 3d av b 9th and 10th sts

Keyser F. M. boarding house, 1116 4th av

Keyser Jennie, res 1116 4th av

Kienla Agnes, res 914 4th av

Kidd Peter, conductor, C. & O. R. R. res 1015 7th av

Kilcoyne Andrew, blacksmith, res 1913 3d av

Kilcoyne John, blacksmith. res 1913 3d av

Kilcoyne Patrick, res 1913 3d av

Kilcoyne Thomas, laborer, res 1913 3d av

Killgore C. W. conductor, res 1139 6th av

Kilgore Hannibal, col'd, teamster, res 727 alley b 3d and 3d avs and 7th and 8th sts

Kimball Laura, res 1321 3d av

King Albert, res 1120 4th av

King Albert W. res 1917 3d av

King C. C. res 1844 5th av

King Charles H. blacksmith, res 1917 3d av

King Mrs. Debbie. col'd, laundress, 727 alley b 2d and 3d avs and 7th and 8th sts

King Ernest, col'd, boot black, res 2d av b 6th and 7th sts

King E. J. wks C. & O. depot, bds 1106 7th av

King Ethel, res 1122 4th av

King Eugene, telegraph operator, res 529 12th st

King Grace, col'd, res alley b 3d and 4th avs and 11th and 12th sts

Kinly Mrs. Tennie, col'd, res 745 3d av

King Netta M. res 1917 3d av

King Rosa, domestic, res 511 10th st

KING W. W. pastor, M. E. Church, res 419 10th st

King T. A. agent, res 1917 3d av

King W. E. attorney and stenographer, 910 3d av

King W. S. trainmaster, res 611 9th st

Kinnaird Carrie, res 805 7th av

Kinnaird Capt. W. A. grocery clerk, res 803 7th av

Kinnaird W. T. clerk Adams Express Co. res 803 7th av

Kinzer J. W. machinist, res 1230 4th av

Kirk Loyd, laborer, res 6 Frame Row

Kirk P. res 1916 Maple av

68   HUNTINGTON [KY] DIRECTORY.

MRS. K. A. KNEFF,

811 THIRD AVENUE,

Keeps Constantly on hand all the Latest Novelties in

MILLINERY, NOTIONS and DRESS GOODS.

All work done in the most approved style by competent
and experienced persons at

POPULAR PRICES.

☞ SPRING and SUMMER OPENING FROM THE 18th to 25th OF APRIL.

Kirkpatrick H. L. physician, 322 9th st, res cor 4th and
    9th st
KIRKPATRICK & NORTHRUP, druggists, 322
    9th st
Kite Milton, moulder, res 8 n Ensign shops
Kestler William, superintendant Electric Light Works,
    res 1007 3d av
Klingle G. F. contractor, res 912 6th av
Kingle Pearl, 912 6th av
KNEFF Mrs. K. A. millinery, 811 3d av, res 809
    3d av
Kneff Lyman P. carpenter, res 809 3d av
Knight Alice, servant, res 2213 3d av
Knight Allen, res 1941 Buffington av
Knight Nola, servant, res 2209½ 3d av
Knight Stella, bds 1936 Maple av
Knight Wesley W. res 1941 Buffington av
Koontz Charles H. farmer, res 1699 8th av
Koontz Charles R. laborer, res 1699 8th av
Koontz Edgar E. moulder, 1699 8th av
Koontz Elijah, laborer, res 1699 8th av
Kothe J. W. baker, 328 9th st
Kuhns Mrs. Josephine, dress maker, res 220 12th st
Kyle E. (E. K. & S. R. Wallace.) Sheriff of Cabell
    County, 702 and 704 3d av, res Cox Landing, West
    Virginia
KYLE & WALLACE, (E. Kyle & S. R. Wallace),
    feed store, 702 and 704 3d av
Kyle Robert L. res 535 9th st
Kyle Will G. flour and feed merchant, 3d av b 7th and
    8th sts, bds 916 5th av

E. KYLE.   S. R. WALLACE.

KYLE & WALLACE,

Mammoth Feed Store.

All Goods in their line kept in Large Quantities, and sold
WHOLESALE AND RETAIL. Headquarters for

LIME, ÷ CEMENT, ÷ HAIR, ÷ HAY, ÷ STRAW

Corn, Oats, Meal, Salt, and all kinds of
Ground Feed. Sole Agents for

HARTER'S A 1 FLOUR,

THE BEST IN THE WORLD, AND

Toledo STEAM COOKED FEED.

Nos. 702 & 704 Third Ave.,

HUNTINGTON, W. VA.

L

Lackland Mrs. F. T. res 728 4th av
Lacock B. F. plastering contractor, res 517 3d av
Lacock Cash P. res 517 3d av
Lacock D. K. salesman, res 3d av b 5th and 6th sts.
Lacock Daniel P. clerk, 517 3d av
Lacock J. F. plasterer, res 517 3d av
Lacy William H. H. cooper, res 10 Buffington Row
Larsh C. conductor, bds 523 10th st
Lagwood Clara, cook, res 1117 5th av
Laidley A. U. res 1210 3d av
Laidley John B. attorney, 1210 3rd av
Laidley Mrs. Miriam, res 1210 3d av
Lair J. H. lumber inspector, bds 1517 3d av
Lair S. J. car builder, bds 1829 3d av
Lake David, teamster, res 2229 3d av
Lake Martin, clerk, res 330 9th st
Lake John, carpenter, res 29 Buffington Row
Lakin Rev. C. H. Presiding Elder of M. E. Church, res
     923 6th av
Lakin Lessie, res 923 6th av
Lakin William, student, 923 6th av
Lallance Anna M. teacher, res 1687 8th av
Lallance Bertie F. res 1687 8th av
Lallance Charles N. painter, res 1687 8th av
Lallance Ethel B. res 717 4th av
Lallance J. B. carpenter, 1009 7th av
Lallance Mrs. M. A. milliner, 913½ 3d av res same
Lallance M. F. painter, res 717 4th av

Lallance R. S. sign writer and decorator, 3d av b 8th and
9th sts, res 918 4th av
Lallance Lue, res 918 4th av
Lambert E. B. printer, bds Merchants' Hotel
Lambert Isaac, 519 20th st
Lambert John F. wks Ensign Co. res 519 20th st
Lambert William, laborer, res West Huntington
Lancaster Susan, cook, res 314 9th st
Landress A. T. carpenter, res 415 11th st
Landress Fannie, res 415 11th st
Landress Lizzie, res 415 11th st
Landress Minnie, res 415 11th st
Lane Mrs. Ann, res 518 11th st
Lane Julia E. res 1937 Buffington av
Lane Leonora, res 1937 Buffington av
Lane William, machinist, res 1736 8th av
Lane W. H. wks Ensign Co. res 1937 Buffington av
Lang Lewis, laborer, res 1926 5th av
Langdon L. T. candy manufacturer, 317 9th st, res same
Langdon Mrs L. T. res 317 9th st
Langley Susan, res 822 3d av
Lanthorn John, laborer, res 1928 Buffington av
Larison Ella, res 1110 4th av
Lawson John, wks C. & O. shops, bds 737 2d av
Lason John, waiter, res 414 9th st
Lawhorn Jennie, res 1144 4th av
Lawrence Patrick, laborer, res 823 7th av
Layden Michel, wks Ensign Co. 2113 3d av
Layton Anna, res 723 6th av
Lea Mrs. Kate W. res 1018 6th av

L. W. LEETE,

Civil Engineer and Surveyor,

Michael Block, Third Avenue.

HUNTINGTON.

Leake Bettie, res 1819 8th av
Leake J. C. fireman, res 1821 8th av
Lee Alice A. res 1940 8th av
Lee Emma E. res 1940 8th av
Lee Frank. blacksmith, res 1940 8th av
Lee George. brakeman. res 414 9th st
Lee John F. laborer, res 1940 8th av
Lee J W. carpenter, res 415 11th sts
Lee Prof. James M. Sup't Public Schools, res 1342 6th
  av
Lee John, carpenter, bds 913 4th av
Lee John. carpenter, res 1125 4th av
Lee John. painter, res 1847 3d av
Lee Maggie Mrs. col'd. res 1133 3d av
Lee Maurice. clerk, 1111 3d av
LEETE L. W. Civil Engineer and Surveyor, Michael
  Block. 3d av
Lefkowitch L. dry goods and notions. 912 3d av
Legee Henry. painter, res 6 Beardsley Row
Leist Alexander T. (Douthit & L.) saddles and harness, 407
  9th st, res 619 9th st
Leitch Miss Frankie, dressmaker. res 739 4th av
Lemasters Millie, res 2d av b 8th and 9th sts
Lemley Belle, coffee and spice packer, res 8th av b 13th
  and 14th sts
Lemley Isaac, wks Ensign Co. res North Ensign
Lemley Miss Suiter, res 8th st b 2d and 3d avs
Lennes Charles, stenographer, res 529 12th st
Leonard Adam J. tinner. res 1136 3d av
Leonard John, tailor, 905 3d av, bds cor 6th av and
  9th st

Leroy Frank P. dealer in fruit and confectionery, 931 3d av, res 1037 6th av

Leroy J. V. dealer in fruit and confectionery, 915 3d av, res 10th st b 3d and 4th av

Leroy James B. store keeper, res 309 10th st

LeSage J. C. book-keeper, res s s 7th av b 9th and 10th sts

LeSage Dr. I. R. physician, 916 3d av, bds 7th av Hotel

Lester Annie, res 722 6th av

Lester Charles A. painter, res 722 6th av

Lester & Co. restaurant, 834 3d av,

Lester C. E. painter, res 722 6th av

Lester E. (L. & Co.) restaurant, 834 3d av, res same

Lester F. W. photographer, res 722 6th av

Lester Harvey, (L. & Co.) restaurant, 834 3d av, res same

Levin S. merchant, 1004 3d av

Levisa Miss Florence. col'd. res 1951 Locust av

Levisy Foster, col'd. hod carrier. res 1225 3d av alley

Levy Joseph, shoe dealer, 920 3d av, res 1115½ 3d av

Levy Leon. clerk, res 946 4th av

Lewis Charley, laborer, res 222 8th st

Lewis Charles, machinist, res 1049 4th av

Lewis Z. L. col'd, laborer, res 834 7th av

Lewis Hattie, res 1049 4th av

Lewis J. F. carpenter, res 742 4th av

Lewis J. M. stone mason, res n s 4th av, West Huntington

Lewis Jerry, col'd, cook, res 406 9th st

Lewis Lena, col'd, domestic, res 1016 6th av

Lewis Mrs. Mary A. res 222 8th st

Lewis Mrs. S. F. res 26 Buffington Row

Lewis Rev. Samuel K. minister Jewish Synagogue, res 1127 6th av

Lenis Vie, res 941 3d av

Lewis Wiley, res 914 3d av

Liggins N. G. col'd, laborer, res 1951 8th av

Liggins Thomas, col'd, wks Ensign Co. res 1925 8th av

Likens D. J. conductor, res 2209 3d av

Lineburg Bert, painter, bds 926 6th av

Lindle William, engineer, res 1924 6th av

Lingafelt —— book keeper, bds 919 6th av

Lingafelt Guy, book keeper. bds 319 9th st

Lite Mrs. Mary, res s s 3d av, West Huntington

Littleton Charles, laborer, res 1736 5th av

74   HUNTINGTON [LYO] DIRECTORY.

Litten James, shoe maker, res 2 Buffington Row
Littleton John, laborer, res 1736 5th av
Littleton William H. blacksmith, res 1736 5th av
Lloyd C. E. flour packer, res 843 3d av
Lokey William L. clerk, res 853 3d av
Long Charles, laborer, res s s 3d av alley, West Huntington
Long George, blacksmith, res 1738 College av
Long Jacob, blacksmith, res 1703 4th av
Long John, res 1738 College av
Long Sarah, res 1738 College av
Lord J. P. auditor, C. & O. R. R. res 940 7th av
Lottin George, printer, bds 3d av b 9th and 10th sts
Louden Charles, car builder, bds 1007 3d av
Louden Lewis, car builder, bds 1007 3d av
Louderback Emma M. bds 1036 6th av
Louderback Mrs. Isabell, res 1036 6th av
Louderback Mrs. P. res 1036 6th av
Lowden J. A. car builder, res 2205 3d av
Lowery A. C. clerk, res 941 3d av
Lowman C. B. tinner, res 1699 8th av
Lowman L. B. laborer, res 1699 8th av
Loyd George H. miller, res 848 3d av
Loyd Mary, res 848 3d av
Luh Mrs. Mary, res 422 17th st
Lukin Anna, res 923 6th av
Lundy Ellen, res 505 20th st
Lunsford Gordon, blacksmith, res 1931 Buffington av
Lusher Lena, domestic, res 1026 6th av
Lusher Florence A. res 4 Frame Row
Lusher Grace L. res 4 Brick Row
Lusher Leota, res 4 Frame Row
Lusher Myrtle, res 4 Frame Row
Lusher M. M. coffee and spice packer, 1016 3d av, res 8th av b 23d and 24th sts
Lusher Toliver S. laborer, res 4 Frame Row
Lykens Henry, laborer, res 1848 Virginia av
Lykens Scott, laborer, res 1813 Virginia av
Lykens W. T. teamster, res 1813 Virginia av
Lynch G. W. engineer, res 1039 3d av
Lyons Charles J. steam fitter, res 1836 4th av
Lyons Henry, watchman, Gordons Saw Mill
Lyons Mrs. Mary N. res 1137 3d av
Lyons W. H. cashier Ensign Manuf Co. res 1339 4th av

W. H. BULL & SON,

LIVERY

FEED AND SALE STABLE.

HENRY'S OLD STAND,

Ninth St. bet. 2d & 3d Ave.

HUNTINGTON, W. VA.

Special Attention Given to Funerals

D. P. ADAMS.   C. F. COLE.

D. P. ADAMS & CO.

— PRACTICAL —

PLUMBERS,

Steam and Gas Fitters,

— AND DEALERS IN —

PIPE,
PIPE FITTINGS,

RANGES.

Steam, Water and Hot Air
HEATERS,

For Public and Private
Buildings.

Brass Goods

PLUMBERS,
GAS AND STEAM
FITTERS

SUPPLIES.

Take and Execute all Contracts in a Substantial and Workman-like Manner.

No. 1115 THIRD AVENUE,

HUNTINGTON, W. VA.

Millender & Bierman, 1113 Third Ave.
FLOORING, WEATHERBOARDING & MOULDING.

M

McAboy Charles, laborer, res 1920 Locust av
McAboy Miss C. L. res 1910 Locust av
McAboy I. E. machinist, res 1910 Locust av
McAboy O. B. carpenter, res 1910 Locust av
McAboy Thomas, 1910 Locust av
McAluvey Mrs. Mary, res 817 4th av alley
McAlhattan Frank, fireman, res 1133 6th av
McAlhattan William, brakeman, res 1133 6th av
McAllister William, fireman, res 26 Buffington Row
McCALLEN & THUMA, (W. M. M. & T. J. T.) furniture and upholstering, 318 9th st
McCallen W. M. (McC. & Thuma.), upholsterer, bds 804 4th av
McCammos T. J. jailer, 416½ and 418 9th st, res same
McCammos Walter, surveyor, res 416½ and 418 9th st
McCammos Warren, clerk, res 416½ and 418 9th st
McCann Miss B. G. studio, rms 821 6th av
McCarthy B. H. machinist, res 1132 7th av
McCarthy Cora, res 1132 7th av
McCarthy Georgie A. res 1132 7th av
McCaw James, machinist, bds 641 5th av
McCaw M. H. machinist, res 1123 4th av
McCaw W. B. clerk, res 3d av b 9th and 10th sts
McChesney Lizzie, assistant teacher, Marshall College
McClane John C. carpenter, res 1801 4th av
McClary Isaac W. blacksmith, res 1941 4th av
McClintock Ida R. res 1132 4th av
McClintock C. A. manuf stave and lumber, res 1132 4th av
McClintock Herbert D. res 1132 4th av
McClintock Pliny J. res 1132 4th av
McClintock Willie, stage manager Bon Ton, bds Merchant's Hotel
McClintock William R. res 1132 4th av
McClung J. C. express messenger, res 1019 4th av
McClung Lida, res 529 12th st
McClung Mary F. res 1019 4th av
McClung T. W. 1019 4th av
McClure C. W. boiler maker, res 1852 4th av
McClure C. W. Jr. laborer, res 1852 4th av
McCoach John, clerk, res 1125 4th av
McCoach J. M. bill clerk, rms 1125 4th av
McColgan Charles T. res 1834 5th av

McColgan James J. painter, res 1834 5th av
McColgan John W. res 1834 5th av
McCollister D. teamster, res 1123 3d av
McComack A. C. machine hand, res 1720 8th av
McComack Miss Eddie, res 1132 3d av
McComack Mrs. Ethel, res 1130 3d av
McComack Mrs. S. J. res 1132 3d av
McComack W. W. telegraph operator, res 1130 3d av
McComack Scott, res 1720 8th av
McComas George J. attorney at law, Ward Block, res 856 St. Cloud
McCormick Ella, res 929 5th av
McCormick J. E. res 929 5th av
McCormick J. W. teacher, res 1132 3d av
McCown A. grocer, 3d av
McCoy Mrs. Annie W. bds 3d av b 13th and 14th sts
McCoy Dr. C. W. (Saunders & McC.), physician and surgeon, rms 825 5th av

McCoy Samuel E. (Buffington McC. & Co.), shoe merchant, 933 3d av, bds 1342 3d av
McCrady James, blacksmith, res 513 3d av
McCready Mrs. Kate, res 513 3d av
McCready J. W. blacksmith, res 1140 4th av
McCready Mrs. S. V. res 1140 4th av
McCreary J. C. conductor, res 1114 6th av
McCullough Anna H. res 353 4th av
McCullough Rob C. insurance agent, 903 3d av
McCULLOUGH F. F. Clerk County Court, res 1026 6th av
McCullough G. W. stationary engineer, res 1015 7th av
McCullough Henry, clerk, 934 3d av
McCullough Miss Hope, res 353 4th av
McCullough Julius, res cor 4th av and 4th st
McCullough Ollie, type writer, res 1015 7th av
McCullough P. H. Jr., drug clerk, res 353 4th av
McCurdy Benjamin J. coffee roaster, res 848 3d av
McCurdy C. H. student, bds 2213 3d av
McCurdy J. F. foreman, res 3d av b 8th and 9th sts
McDaniel F. C. engineer, res 1029 7th av
McDanniels Mrs. Laura, dress maker, res 1835 4th av
McDonald George E. (Vinson & McD.), attorney, 221½ 10th st, rns same
McDonald Mary, music teacher, bds 1018 6th av
McDermott G. M. notary public, 856 3d av, res Central City, West Virginia
McDonald Sadie, res n 24th st
McDome C. B. passenger conductor, res 827 7th av
McDowell James, carpenter, res 1820 5th av
McDowell J. E. carpenter, res 617 10th st
McDowell John, conductor, res 1218 7th av
McFeters William, col'd, laborer, 905 3d av
McGee Jennie, res 2 Beardsley Row
McGee Reuben, brakeman, res 2 Beardsley Row
McGee Solomon, col'd, wks C. & O. shops, bds 1660 8th av
McGettigan Mrs. Isabella, res 1133 6th av
McGinnis F. J. (Roadcap & McG.), saloon keeper, 327 9th st, res same
McGinnis Hon. Ira J. attorney at law, cor 3d av and 9th st, res 1003 7th av
McGinnis L. B. salesman, res 730 4th av
McGilathery L. S. bolt maker, res 1442 3d av
McGraw Mattie, dining room girl, res 7th av Hotel

McGuire Jennie, col'd, res 1670 8th av

McIlveen Mrs. Agnes, res 420 19th st

McINTOSH GEORGE C. local editor Gazette, 845 3d av, res 810 7th av

McINTOSH G. R. editor Gazette, 845 3d av, res 810 7th av

McKee William, carpenter, res 1906

•McKenderee George, civil engineer, res Central City

McKenna James, brick mason, bds 743 alley b 7th and 8th sts and 4th and 5th avs

McKeny W. L. conductor, res 1421 R. R.

McKiney Archie, (S. B. Morgan & Co.), grocer, 1023 3d av, res Cold Valley, West Virginia

McKinney D. barber, rms 10th st b 2d and 3d avs

McKinney Nettie, col'd, res 801 8th st

McKinney M. T. col'd, Principal City Colored School, res 801 8th st

McLain Joseph E. axle maker, res n 24th st

McLaine Elmer, axle maker, res 505 20th st

McLaughlin Miss Louie, res 1104 7th av

McLaughlin George E. machinist, res 1104 7th av

McLaughlin James S. carpenter, res 1104 7th av

McLaughlin H. R. engineer, bds 641 5th av

McLaughlin James, saloon keeper, 310 9th st, res Guyandotte

McLaughlin Maggie L. school teacher, res 1104 7th av

McLean James C. painter, res 1116 3d av

McLellon J. L. ticket agent, res 730 3d av

McLellon Mrs. K. M. res 730 3d av

McLellon Mrs. M. J. dress maker, 324 9th st, res 730 3d av

McMahon John, blacksmith, bds 2335 8th av

McPherson Charles, col'd, waiter, Florentine Hotel

McPherson Virginia, res b 2d and 3d avs and 7th and 8th sts

McVey Mrs. Mary, boarding house, 1215 3d av

McVicker J. F. moulder, res 1907 4th av

McWilliams R. W. saloon, 909 3d av, res cor 4th av and 14th st

Macumber R. P. carpenter, 815 7th av

Maddy Anna M. res 1238 4th av

Maddy Edward F. framer, res 1238 4th av

Maddy Lizzie B. res 1238 4th av

Maddux J. M. blacksmith helper, res 749 alley b 7th and 8th sts and 3d and 4th av

Maddux Mary, res 749 alley b 7th and 8th sts and 3d and
    4th avs
Madison Mrs. col'd, cook, res 901 6th av
Magee C. C. painter, res 926 6th av
Mallory Samuel, shipping clerk, 1016 3d av, res 3d av b
    10th and 11th sts
Malone P. H. engineer, res 937 7th av
Manggrum James, col'd, brakeman, res 1533 8th av
Manggrum Maria, col'd, res 1533 8th av
Mann Annie, res 844 3d av
Mann Mrs. Carrie, school teacher, res 1356 3d av
Mann D. E. grocery clerk, rms 1316 4th av
Mann Edgar, clerk, res 801 7th av
Mann Mrs. Ella, res 844 3d av
Mann Marion, laborer, res 3 Burks' Row
Mann Thomas O. carpenter contractor, res 844 3d av
Mansfield Mrs. Emma, dress maker, res 622 8th st
Manson Cyrus, col'd, porter, res 816 8th av
Manson Si. porter, 406 9th st
MARCUM & PEYTON, (J. S. M. & T. W. P.), attor-
    neys, 328¾ 9th st

MARSHALL COLLEGE

⇒❋ THE STATE NORMAL SCHOOL. ❋⇐

Third Avenue, Between Sixteenth and Seventeenth Streets.

FACULTY:

THOMAS E. HODGES, A. M., Principal.

MISS MABELLE SCOTT, B. S.

MISS LIZZIE McCHESNEY, L. I. } Assistants.

MISS LULU STEWART,

MRS. F. S. BOWN, Music.

MISS HALLIE WYATT, Drawing.

EXECUTIVE COMMITTEE:

A. F. SOUTHWORTH, Pres.   C. B. HARROLD, Sec'y.

GEO. F. MILLER, Jr., Treas.

HUNTINGTON [MAT] DIRECTORY. 83

Marcum John S. attorney at law, 9th st P. O. Building, res 626 10th st

Marcum J. H. (Kennett & M.), livery and sale stable, 714 and 716 3d av, bds St. Nicholas Hotel

Marks Belda, res 1925 4th av

Marks John W. foreman, res 1925 4th av

Marpoe Samuel, painter, res 2229½ 3d av

Marr B. W. (Emmons & M.), wholesale hardware, 902 3d av, res 609 9th st

Marr J. L. (Wirthlin & M.), prop. wharf boat, foot of 10th st, rms s s 3d av b 9th and 10th sts

Marrs G. S. machinist, res 3d av b 7th and 8th sts

Marshall Allen, laborer, res 2251 8th av

MARSHALL COLLEGE, the State Normal School, 3d av b 16th and 17th sts. Thomas E. Hodges, A. M. Principal

Marshall Lulu, col'd, servant, 1309 3d av

Marshall N. F. minister, Episcopal Church, res 518 11th st

Martin Addie, res 405 20th st

Martin B. O. res 405 20th st

Martin Benjamin O. butcher, res 1948 College av

Martin Ellen, res 1116 3d av alley

Martin Elmer, wks planing mill, res 1341 4th av

Martin Mrs. Eveline, res 1921 3d av

MARTIN G. B. planing mill, res 1341 4th av

Martin George E. laborer, res 9 Frame Row

Martin George O. laborer, res 2221 3d av

Martin George O. laborer, res 1948 College av

Martin John D. laborer, res 9 Frame Row

Martin Miss R. F. res 9 Frame Row

Martin W. H. res 405 20th st

MARTIN ZENAS, editor Babtist Banner, 930½ 4th av, res 1522 3d av

Masey Alex, asst. wharf master, res 1014 6th av alley

Massey Alexander, boat watchman, res 1014 6th av alley

Massey Mrs. Maggie, res 1123 3d av

Massie Adam, laborer, res 1925 3d av

Massie Lewis, wks Ensign Co. res 1925 3d av

Massie Nathan, wks Ensign Co. res 1925 3d av

Mason Robert, wks Ensign Co. bds 1815 Virginia av

Mather Mrs. A. G. 1313 3d av

Mather O. W. res 1313 3d av

Matheny Cora, res 825 2d av

Matheny Joseph H. carpenter, res s s 3d av, West Huntington

Matheny William, carpenter, res 825 2d av

Matier William, blacksmith, res 1343 3d av

Mathews Anna L res 1730 8th av

Mathews C. wks Ensign Co. res 1240 3d av

Mathews D. E. attorney at law, 835 3d av, bds St Nicholas Hotel

Mathews Emma, res 1722 4th av

MATHEWS & HUMPHREYS, (S. V. M. & L. W. H.) photographers, 948 3d av

Matthews Joseph, car builder, res 1735 4th av

Matthews Joseph E. photographer, res 715 6th av

Matthews J. W. carpenter, C. & O. bds Continental Hotel

Matthews J. W. carpenter, Ensign Co. res 1722 4th av

Matthews Mrs. Laura, res 6th av b 7th and 8th sts

Matthews Mrs. M. J. res 717 6th av

Matthews M. M. machinist, res 1730 8th av

Matthews M. T. car inspector, res 1730 8th av

MATTHEWS R. A. prop. Florentine Hotel

Matthews Samuel, (M. & Humphreys) photographer, 948 3d av, res 723 6th av

Matthews S. V. photographer, 3d av, res 723 6th av

Maupin C. W. res 1346 4th av

May Minnie, dress maker, res 1119 3d av

Mayenchein William, machinist, res 1822 4th av

Mayes J. W. car builder, res 1715 Virginia av

Maynard Alifare, washing, 810 alley b 8th and 9th sts, and 2d and 3d avs

Mayo Lucy, col'd, washing, res 1117 4th av alley

Mayo M. L. physician, 942 and 944 5th av, res same

Mayo Susan, res 942 and 944 5th av
Maypes Charles, car builder, bds 101 24th st
Mays Dora, res 3 Beardsley Row
Mays George, res 3 Beardsley Row
Mays Part, laborer, res 3 Beardsley Row
Mazeen Mrs. Agnes S. res 1020 7th av
Mead John, barber, res 708 9th st
Meadows William, car builder, res 324 18th st
Meadows Eugene, res 1955 Virginia av
Meadows Flora E. res 1722 8th av
Meadows H. W. bar keeper, 1017 3d av, bds w s 9th st b
4th and 5th avs
Meadows J. H. carpenter, res 1722 8th av
Meadows Lewis, machinist, 1933 Maple av
Meadows Mary M. res 1722 8th av
Meadows Nannie, house keeper, Pleasant View
Meadows Sophia. cook. res 1123 6th av
MEDFORD THOMAS, coal merchant, res 809, 811
and 813 5th av
Meek Lewis C. car builder, res 1723 Virginia av
Messenger Alma, res 1754 4th av
Messenger Gertrude, res 1754 4th av
Messenger H. D. carpenter, res 1754 4th av
Messersmith Lelle, res 1934 7th av
Messersmith Robert, blacksmith, res 1934 7th av
Messersmith R. R. carpenter, bds 926 6th av
Meyers Benjamin F. Sr. engineer, res 1027 7th av
Meyers B. F. Jr fireman, res 1027 7th av
Meyers C. H. teamster, res 209 7th st
Meyers Mrs. Roxie. res 209 7th st
Michaels Charles E. res 1109½ 3d av
Michaels J. F. res 1109½ 3d av
Mickens John, boiler maker, res 414 9th st
Mickens Nora, res 414 9th st
Mickie T. L. attorney, 1013 5th av
Mickle C. machinist, res 1138 4th av
Mickle Mrs. Hattie E. res 1133 4th av
Middlekauff Elmer, book-keeper, bds 916 3d av
Middlesworth C. farmer, res 921 7th av
Middlesworth Lenia, res 921 7th av
Middlesworth Roxie, res 921 7th av
Middleton J. E. student, res 1801 3d av
Middleton William J. clerk, res 1801 3d av
Midkiff Gordon, watchman, res 903 2d av

86   HUNTINGTON [MIL] DIRECTORY.

Midkiff Robert, laborer, res 903 2d av
Midkiff Solomon, wks C. & O. shops, res 15 Buffington
  Row
Miles L. S. wks Ensign Co. res 1915 5th av
Miles Mrs. June, res 36 Buffington Row
Miles Mrs. L. res 36 Buffington Row
Miles Verna, domestic, res 925 3d av
Miller Albert M. brakeman. res 1655 8th av
Miller C. A. wks Jackson's saw mill, res 1947 Locust av
Miller C. G. wks ensign Co. res 313 19th st
Miller E. M. engineer, res 1809 8th av
Miller Mrs. E. M. dress maker, res 1123 3d av
Miller Edward W. res 101 24th st
Miller Fannie, res 1947 Locust av
Miller George, res 1809 8th av
MILLER GEO. F. Jr. Vice-President First National
  Bank, res 1056 4th av
Miller Isaac, col'd, barber, bds 2d av b 8th and 9th sts
Miller J. H Jr. traveling salesman, res 3d av b 10th and
  11th sts
Miller J. S. pattern maker, res 1941 6th av
Miller J. T. laborer, res 1947 Locust av
Miller Mamie, res 1947 Locust av
Miller Mary, cook, res 1019 4th av
Miller O. domestic, res 1030 4th av
Miller S. S carpenter, res 1904 Locust av
Miller Sterling, brakeman, col'd, bds 819 2d av
Miller Willie, res 1947 Locust av
Miller Miss Willie, res 1725 8th av
Miller William, engineer, bds 636 10th st
Miller William, wks Ensign Co. res 412 17th st
Miller William C. (Harrold & M.) insurance and real es-
  tate agent, 920 3d av, res Central City
Miller W. F. laborer, res 1947 Locust av
MILLENDER & BIERMAN, planing mill and
  building contractors, 1106, 1108, 1110 and 1112 3d
  av
Millender C. F. merchant and contractor, 1113 3d av, res
  1127 4th av
Miles D. H. col'd, cook, res 1117 4th av alley
Miles Jackson, col'd, railroader, bds 1660 8th av
Miles J. L. wks Ensign Co. 1942 Locust av
Miles J. P. machine hand, res 1939 Locust av
Miles S. O. machine hand, res 1922 Maple av

Millslagle Fred, machinist, bds 926 6th av
Miller Mrs. Annie, res 724 6th av
Minier. P. G. car builder, res 1718 5th av
Mitchell A. M. carpenter, res 1755 4th av
Mitchell A. P. City Marshall, res n s 4th av, West Huntington
Mitchell Demma, school teacher, res 1755 4th av
Mitchell Effie B. domestic, res 1845 8th av
Mitchell Mrs. E. M. n s 4th av, West Huntington
Mitchell H. M. conductor, res 726 6th av
Mitchell Maud, res n s 4th av, West Huntington
Mitchell Mattie V. n s 4th av, West Huntington
Mitchell Walter D. res 726 6th av
Mobus George E. assistant foreman Ensign Co. res 1527 3d av
Molter C. res 1113½ 3d av
Molter Elizabeth, bakery, 831 2d av. res same
Molter L. A. res 1113½ 3d av
Molter Louis, bakery, 831 3d av, res same
Molter Kate, res 1113½ 3d av
Molter Phebe, res 1113½ 3d av
Molter W. C. bakery, 831 3d av. res same
Monroe Mary, col'd. res s s 3d av West Huntington
Monroe Robert, col'd, teamster, s s 3d av, West Huntinton
Monroe William G. wks Ensign Co. 1219 3d av
Montague John, carpenter, res 1956 Locust av
Moor James G. machinist, res 227 24th st
Moor Jennie R. res 225 and 227 24th st
Moor Mary D. res 225 and 227 24th st
Moore A. B. printer, res 1125 4th av
Moore D. J. freight conductor, res 753 4th av
Moore Jack, col'd, bar tender, res 8th st b 2d and 3d avs
Moore Jennie, coffee and spice packer, res 3d av b 23 and 24th sts
Moore Jessie. res 753 4th av
Moore Mrs. Martha, col'd, res 8th st b 2d and 3d avs
Moore Minnie E. res 1031 6th av
Moore William D. machinist, res 1031 6th av
Mootz Frederick, wks Ensign Co. res 1951 4th av
Mootz Jacob wks Ensign Co. res 1831 4th av
Mootz Mary, waiter. res 1104 3d av
More F. H. res 712 4th av

DAN A. MOSSMAN,

THE LEADING COAL AND ICE DEALER.

My COAL is all handled with forks and Re-screened after coming to my yard. Call and see me.

Office. Second Avenue and Eighth Street.-

Also HOUSES FOR RENT.

Moses J H, carpenter, res 1829 8th av
Motz Phebe, 1120 4th av
Moreland A. H. carpenter, res 1118 4th av
Moreland F. W. carpenter, res 819 7th av
Moreland Carrie, res 713 3d av
Moreland Edgar, machinist, bds 713 3d av
Moreland Lida, dress maker, res 713 3d av
Moreland Nancy B. res 713 3d av
Moreland Robert, engineer, res Shelton's Addition
Moreland W. H. car builder, res 1333 12th av alley
Morford Thomas, boiler maker C. & O. shops
Morgan S. B. (S. B. M. & Co.) grocer, 1023 3d av
Morepoe Sam R. painter, res 2229 3d av
Morris George, carpenter, res 1221 14th st
Morris John, carpenter, res 1221 14th st
Morris Kate, cook, res 1128 3d av
Morris Lindsey, clerk, bds 1018 6th av
Morris Robert, engineer, res 913 4th av
Morris Miss Willie, res 1221 14th st
Morris William, porter, res 406 9th st
Morrison Joel, laborer, res alley b 3d and 4th avs and 11th and 12th st
Morrell Benjamin, carpenter, res 913 4th av
Morrow Charles H. carpenter, res 1105 4th av
Morrow R. G. carpenter, res 17 Frame Row
Morton Mrs. Sarah, res 1533 8th av
MOSSMAN D. A. coal dealer, cor 2d av and 8th st, res 925 5th av
Mowrey John W. carpenter, bds 8 Frame Row
Moyle William, wks Ensign Co. 1956 8th av

Mulhallen J. R. yard master, res 706 9th st
Mullen Etta, res 2109 3d av
Mullen Joseph, car builder, res 2109 3d av
Mullens J. D. teamster, res West Huntington
Mullineaux A. A. fireman, bds 641 5th av
Murphy Adelia, res 841 4th av
Murphy Delia, res 4th av b 8th and 9th st
Myers Mrs. Mercena, res 1118½ 4th av
Myers Charles, col'd, house boy, 1141 and 1143 3d av
Myers G. H. attorney and City Recorder, res 9th st b 6th
and 7th avs
Myers Joseph, blacksmith, res 2311 8th av
Myers J. D. physician, 9th st b 6th and 7th avs
Myers Henry J. conductor, res 9th st b 6th and 7th avs.
Myers Mrs. Mary E. res 711 6th av
Myers Mary L. M. school teacher, res 9th st b 6th and 7th
avs
Myers Sallie, dressmaker, res 711 6th av

N

Nagle A. H. engineer, res 1018 7th av
Nance John, engineer, res 5 North Ensign Shops
Nash Charles, book-keeper, res 1417 & 1419 6th av
Nash Frank A. queensware dealer, 3d av b 8th and 9th
sts., res 817 6th av.
Neal Thomas, plasterer, res 1926 Locust av
Neal Charles, plasterer, s s 3d av W Huntington
Neal George I. attorney at law, 222 10th st, rms N E cor
3d av and 10th st
Neff Lewis, machine hand, res 1905 5th av
Nelson T. E. traveling salesman, rms 907 3d av
Nelson T. L. bds 1421 R R
Nesperby Charles, machinist, res 1119 3d av
Nesperly Mrs. M. J., dress maker, res 1119 3d av
New Elizabeth, res 1021 4th av
New F. A. tinner, res 1020 4th av
Newcomb E. L. engineer, res 1222 4th av
Newcomb L. T. book-keeper, 1222 4th av
Newcomb W. H. Jr. dry goods clerk, res 1222 4th av
Newcomb W. H. Sr. carpenter, res 1222 4th av
Newhart Jack, laborer, bds 416 8th st
Newman America. res 826 4th av
Newman Belle, res 826 4th av

G. A. NORTHCOTT.   P. C. BUFFINGTON.

NORTHCOTT & BUFFINGTON,

CLOTHIERS,

HATTERS and MENS' FURNISHERS.

Merchant Tailoring

A SPECIALTY.

J. SCHEIVLEY, - Manager and Cutter.

---

905 THIRD AVE.,

HUNTINGTON, W. VA.

Newman Miss C. clerk, res 524 8th st
Newman Clara, clerk, res 5th av b 9th and 10 sts
Newman Emma, res 826 4te av
Newman Florence, res 311 21st st
Newman H. dry goods and notions, 914 3d av, res 5th av
    b 9th and 10 th sts
Newman Henry, laborer, res 318 21st st
Newman Irvin, carpenter, res 526 8th st
Newman John, laborer, res 318 21st st
Newman Leonidas H. salesman, res 826 4th av
Newman Leroy, salesman, res 4th av b 8th and 9th sts
Newman Miss M. clerk, res 3d av b 7th and 8th sts
Newman Mertie, res 826 4th av
Newsome Byron, col'd, laborer, res 1 Beardsley Row
Newsome Joe, col'd, res 1 Beardsley Row
Newsome Nannie, col'd, 1 Beardsley Row
Newsome Ruth, res 1 Beardsley Row
Newson Virgie, domestic, res 912 6th av
Newton Amanda, laundress, res 817 4th av alley
Newton Fanny, laundress, res 817 4th av alley
Newton Otis, clerk, 817 4th av alley
Newton Sylvester, miller, res 817 4th av alley
Newton Toka, laundress, res 817 4th av alley
Nicely W. D. car builder, res 1919 Maple av
Nichol Zella, res s s 6th av b 9th and 10th sts
Nicholas Dolly, laundress, res 846 3d av rear
Nicholas George, 941 3d av
NICHOLAS WM. A. assistant pastor 3d av Baptist
    church, res 427 10th st
Nicholas M. J. machinist, res 10 Brick Row
Nichols Zilla, domestic, res 911 6th av
NICKESON MARTIN & CO. dealers in lumber,
    foot of 14th st, res 1334 4th av
Nichols George, col'd, waiter, res alley b 3d and 4th av
    and 11th and 12th sts
Niday James, laborer, res 1849 4th av
Noonan Mrs. Ellen, res 1829 3d av
Noonan Mrs. Lizzie, boarding house, res 1829 3d av
Noonan Mary, res 1829 3d av
Norris Ed, col'd, res 5 West Buffington Row
Norris Harriet, col'd, res 5 West Buffington Row
Norris J. B. machinist, res 717 6th av
Norris Thomas, car builder, res 1942 8th av
NORTHCOTT & BUFFINGTON, (G. A. N. & P.
    C. B.) clothiers, 905 3d av

MARTIN NICKESON & CO.

Wholesale and Retail Dealer in all
kinds of

ROUGH AND DRESSED

LUMBER!

Building Materials of All Kinds.

CONTRACTORS AND BUILDERS.

Will furnish any and everything necessary for
the completion of buildings on short notice.

Office and Mill at Foot of Fourteenth Street,

RIVER BANK.

Northcott G. A. (N. & Buffington) clothiers, 905 3d av, bds
531 9th st
Northrup C. L. conductor, res 1714 8th av
Northrup Mary E. rer 1714 8th av
Norton Miss A. E. res 1106 7th av
Norton Cammie, res 1106 7th av
Norton Mary F. res 1106 7th av
Norton Wm. M. machinist, res 529 12th st
Notter J. A. laborer, res 1935 8th av
Notter J. M. carpenter, res 1730 8th av
Notter Oscar, laborer, res 1935 8th av
Nutter Mrs. Berna, res alley 14th st b 2d and 3d av
Nutter Mrs. V. coffee and spice packer, res 14th st b 2d
and 3d av alley

O

Oakes G. W. clerk, res 1928 4th av
O'Beirne Gordon, attorney, 835 3d av, bds St. Nicholas
Hotel

O'Brien Lizzie, rear 4 Burks Row
O'Brien John, laborer, res 609 3d av
O'Brien Mrs. J. C. clerk, res 829 6th av
O'Brien Michael, laborer, res 609 3d av
O'Brien William, laborer, rear 4 Burks Row
Odell James, bell boy, 941 3d av
Ogden Will. L. car inspector, res 1139 6th av
O'Hara Joseph H. tailor and cutter, 854 3d av, bds 124
    3d av
Oliver William, blacksmith, res 2215 3d av
Oliver W. G. painter, res 320 18th st
Olsen John, draughtsman, bds 1356 3d av
O'Neil James, wks Ensign Co. bds 101 24th st
O'Neill Thomas, (Ingram & O'N.), machinist, 949 2d av
ONEY J. K. cashier Bank of Huntington, 1002 3d av,
    res 1304 3d av
Orndorff Charles, fireman, res 904 7th av
Osborn Elvin, tailor, res 1116 3d av
Osborn E. M. tailor, res 3d av b 11th and 12th sts
Osborn W. D. agent, bds 753 and 755 2d av
Osgood H. S. machinist, res 1128 6th av
Oswald Bernhard, bds 1917 5th av
Otterstatter John, res 827 4th av
Otto Sherman, baggage master, bds 641 5th av
OVERBY WARREN, Jr., insurance agent, 856 3d
    av, res 1111 6th av
Overby Warren, Sr., clerk, res 1111 6th av
Overton Charles, col'd, res 1688 8th av
Owen Cynthia, res 1831 Virginia av
Owens Emma, res 1831 Virginia av
Owens Henry T. farmer, res 1835 Virginia av
Owens J. L. laborer, res 1845 8th av
Owens Samuel, res 1831 Virginia av
Owens William, carpenter, res 1831 Virginia av

P

Pack Ida, col'd, chamber maid, 7th av Hotel
Pack Mary, col'd, cook, res alley b 3d and 4th avs and
    11th and 12th sts
Pack Thomas, col'd, wks Ensign Co. res alley b 3d and
    4th avs and 11th and 12th sts
Page A. S. dentist, 809 2d av
Page Cora, stenographer, res 1242 3d av

Page Emma, type writer, bds 940 6th av
Page O. W. dress maker. res 2d av b 8th and 9th sts
Paine F. stenographer, First National Bank, bds 1020 7th
     av
Paine Lidney B. laborer, res 1932 Locust av
Palmer A. B. insurance and real estate agent, 854 3d
     av, res 845 3d av
Palmer Nancy J. res 845 3d av
Palmer Thomas C. foreman, res 828 4th av
Pancake Mrs. Elmer, res 2229 3d av
Pancake William, laborer, res 2229 3d av
Payne James B. freight conductor, res 1217 6th av
Parnell John, painter, res 921½ 2d av
Pannill B. lumber inspector, res 753 3d av
Pannill Jackson L. baggage master, bds 753 3d av
Pannill Jerry W. machinist, bds 753 3d av
Pannill Mary S. res 753 3d av
Pannill Thomas M. grocery clerk, 833 3d av
Parish David H. res 1103 6th av
Parish William J. manager plaster factory, river bank b
     15th and 16th st, res 1103 6th av
Parish Maggie M. res 1114 6th av
Parish Richard B. clerk, res 1103 6th av
Parker J. I. bar tender, res 941 3d av
Parsons Maggie, res 414 9th st
Parsons C. F. retired merchant, res 1639 6th av
Parsons Edward, laborer, res 1915 4th av
Parsons John, wks Ensign Co. bds 6th av b 8th and 9th sts
Parsons Miss Ruth H. res 1639 6th av
Parson T. E. clerk, Continental Hotel, 801 2d av
Parson Mrs. T. E. dress maker, bds Continental Hotel
PARSONS W. E. manuf plaster, office 1329 9th st
Partridge Frank, teamster, bds 631 3d av
Patten Joseph, carpenter, res 1044 4th av
Patterson A. W. painter, res 1922 4th av
Patterson George, errand boy, res 1042 3d av alley
Patterson Lizzie, res 1042 3d av alley
Paul John A. passenger conductor, res 822 6th av
Paul William, conductor, res 1031 7th av
Peaco John, policeman, res cor 2d av and 5th st
Peacock C. train dispatcher, rms 1102 7th av
Peckitt William, laborer, res 1936 8th av
Peeples G. W. carpenter, res 1944 6th av
Pelot J. W. telegrapher, bds 516 9th st

Pelot Nellie, bds 516 9th st
Pemberton Dave, laborer, res 3d av, West Huntington
Pendleton Edward, col'd, wks C. & O. shops, res 830 8th av
Pennypacker Fannie, res 4th av, West Huntington
Pennybacker Mrs. S. H. res 1101 6th av
PEPPER R. H. physician, 411 9th st, res 413 9th st
Perdue D. M. col'd, barber, 832 3d av, res same
Perkins Belle, domestic, res 516 9th st
Perkins Clarence, druggist, res 938 4th av
Perkins Elma, res 1020 7th av
Perkins H. N. telegrapher, res 1020 7th av
Perkins Lallie, res 1020 7th av
Perkins Mary, 1020 7th av
Perkins Mrs. M. B. boarding house, 1107 6th av
PERKINS M. C. & SON, (M. C. P. & C. P.), druggists, 330 9th st
Perkins Rev. R. J. col'd, Baptist minister, St. Albans West Virginia, res 819 2d av
Pernell Nancy, col'd, wash woman, alley b 3d and 4th avs, and 11th and 12th sts
Perry Alice, res 3d av b 11th and 12th sts
Perry E. J. fireman, res 1816 4th av
Perry George, col'd, teamster, res 3d av b 11th and 12th sts
Persinger J. R. car builder, res 1948 College av
Person Elizabeth, domestic, res 317 9th st
Peters Frank, student, res 916 5th av
Peters Harriet, col'd, res 1220 6th av
Peters F. P. col'd, laborer, res n 24th st
Peters J. G. col'd, laborer, res n 24th st
Peters William, col'd, laborer, res n 24th st
Peterson J. J. United States Consul to Honduras, res 1236 3d av
Petit Miss Ethel L. res 1039 6th av
PETIT N. C. dealer in coal and ice, res 1039 6th av
Peyton Charles, col'd, brakeman, res 10 Buffington Row
Peyton Sallie, school teacher, res 1236 4th av
Peyton Mrs. Sarah, res 1236 4th av
Peyton T. W. attorney, 328½ 9th st, res 630 10th st
Peyton Mrs. T. W. res 630 10th st
Pfefer Mrs. Josephine, res 1035½ 7th av
Pheasant Sherman, car builder, bds 1001 3d av
Phenice Earl, car builder, res 2211 3d av
Phenice M. W. laborer, bds 101 24th st

————THE————

FOUNTAIN DRUG STORE

M. C. PERKINS & SON,

PROPRIETORS.

PERFUME,

DRUGS, MEDICINES & CHEMICALS,

A FULL LINE OF

ART MATERIAL

And Studies.

NINTH Street, Opp. Post Office,

HUNTINGTON, W. VA.

HUNTINGTON [POL] DIRECTORY. 97

Phillips H. J. pattern maker, bds 1829 3d av
Phillips Martha, col'd, wks 1303 3d av
Phillips Scott, col'd, res 840 8th av
Pleasants Bert, car builder, res 1719 4th av
Pickins A. A. laborer, res 1840 4th av
Pierce H. civil engineer, res 1131 6th av
Pierce Mary L. res 1131 6th av
Pierce W. A. street car driver, res 216 12th st
Pigman Eva, res 932 7th av
Pigman J. E. grocer, res 932 7th av
PIGMAN MRS. MARY E. lunch room, 901 7th av, res 932 7th av
Pike Rosetta, res 1843 Virginia av
Pilcher Charles, engineer, res 1120 7th av
Pine A. G. telegraph operator, rms 918 4th av
Pine William A. tinner, res 1917 3d av
Pirre L. V. clerk, bds 10th st b 3d and 4th avs
Pinkerman Albert, laborer, res 24 Buffington Row
Pitzer Hattie E. res 641 5th av
Pizzella Mrs. Josephine, res 8th st b 2d and 3d avs
Poage George H. livery stable, 1203 4th av
Poage J. B. City Treasurer, 851 3d av, res 1223 5th av
Poage Mrs. Sarah A. res 1219 5th av
Poar Alfred H. farmer, res 834 7th av
Poar Charles B. clerk, 909 3d av
Poindexter Emma, col'd, res 1670 8th av
Poindexter G. bell boy, Florentine hotel
Poindexter T. X. bell boy, res 1046 3d av alley
Poindexter John, car builder, res 1046 3d av alley
Poindexter Marshall, col'd, switchman, res 1670 8th av
Poindexter W. W. (Goodwin & P.), props Carrollton Hotel, opp C. & O. depot
Point George M. machinist, res 1012 6th av
Point Walter W. foreman, res 1012 6th av
Pollard Eugenia E. res n s 3d av, West Huntington
Pollard Edwin G. baggage master, res n s 3d av, West Huntington
POLLARD JOHN C. coal dealer, res n s 3d av, West Huntington
Pollard Luella S. res n s 3d av, West Huntington
Pollock H. farmer, res 16th st b 6th and 7th avs
Pollock Luther, waiter, res 405 9th st
Pollock Morgan, teamster, res 1948 Buffington av
Pollock Otto, res 16th st b 6th and 7th avs

Pollock Reuben, coffee mixer, res 8th av b 18th and 19th sts
Pollock R. H. carpenter, res 1837 8th av
Pollock Sallie, res 16th st b 6th and 7th avs
Polten Charles, blacksmith, res 2016 4th av
Polten Robert, blacksmith, res 2016 4th av
Poole Mrs. C. M. boarding house, 2113 3d av
Poole Homer W. pipe fitter, 1328 4th av
Poole John, teamster, res 2113 3d av
POORE MARK, pension agent, res 316 9th st
Porter Mrs. Annie, res 818 7th av
Porter Albert N. saloon keeper, 321 9th st, bds 1245 3d av
Potter A. W. bar tender, 319 9th st
POTTS & CAMMACK, (J. N. P. & J. H. C.), Insurance and Real Estate Agents, 324 9th st
POTTS J. N. (P & Cammack) Real Estate and Insurance Agent, and Notary Public, 324 9th st, res 734 3d av
Powell Clara, res 1663 8th av
Parrell William, col'd, barber, res 3d av b 9th and 10th sts
Pratt Frank, upholsterer, res 1533 3d av
Preston C. B. wks Ensign Co. res 322 18th st
Preston E. S. res 322 18th st
PRICE B. K. grocer, 1010 3d av
Price Henry, waiter, res 941 3d av
Price James, col'd, wks C. & O. shops, bds 1660 8th av
Price Mrs. Jane, res 12 Beardsley Row
Price Lulu, res 8 Beardsley Row
Price Nannie, res 8 Beardsley Row
Price Simon, laborer, bds 414 9th st
PRICE MAC T. coal dealer, 1118 3d av, res 914 4th av
Price W. H. col'd, waiter, res 822 7th av alley
Price Alice, res 526 8th av
Prichard C. N. publisher Cricket, res 734 4th av
Prichard Gertrude, res 734 4th av
Prichard Hallie, res 734 4th av
Prichard Mrs. S. A. res 734 4th av
Prichard Warren, laborer, res 1909 Virginia av
Prichard Pattie, domestic, res 1019 5th av
Prickitt Mrs. Emma, rms 940 6th av
Prickitt W. B. cashier Commercial Bank, rms 940 6th av
Priddie B. L. clerk, bds St. Nicholas Hotel
Pride Vic, col'd, cook, res 1117 4th av alley

Kanawha,
Ohio River
—AND—
Kentucky
COAL.

T. M. PRICE
Coal Dealer.

Grate, Stove,
Steam,
—AND—
Anthracite
COAL.

————HANDLES ONLY THE VERY BEST————

COAL & COKE

Lump Nut, Nut and Slack,
Pea and Slack Coal.

I re-screen my Coal at the Yard, and only send out Clean
Coal.   I also handle

BIRD'S EYE CANNEL COAL,

which is clean, free from sulphur, soot and dirt.   This Coal is long
lasting, and I will guarantee it to give satisfaction.   Prompt attention
and quick delivery.

OFFICE, Third Ave. bet. 11th & 12th.

T. M. PRICE.

THE HUNTINGTON TRANSFER CO.

—DOES ALL KINDS OF—

HAULING AND MOVING.

Contracts taken for Filling Lots and Digging Cellars.
Baggage Handled with Care.

WE HAVE LARGE **WARE-ROOM** For STORING Goods

We will be responsible for breakage or loss of goods or freight
left in our care.

T. M. PRICE & CO. Prop.

Office, Third ave. bet. 11th & 12th Sts.

Prime Mary, res 734 3d av
Pringel Ellie, servant, res 1911 Maple av
Primick William, engineer, res b 3d and 4th avs and 9th 10th sts
Pritchard Dr. T. J. (Buffington & P.), physician, res 1135 5th av
Prose I. blacksmith, res 1140 4th av
Provo Anna, res 1822 5th av
Provo Cora, res 1822 5th av
Provo Peter, carpenter, res 1822 5th av
Puthuff H. S. carpenter, res s s 3d av, West Huntington
Puthuff James M. contractor, res 823 2d av
Puthuff Miss J. M. (P. & Terrell), milliner, 1027 3d av, res s s 2d av b 8th and 9th sts
Puthuff John W. carpenter, res s s 3d av, West Huntington
Puthuff Jennie, milliner, res 823 2d av
Puthuff Lydia, milliner, res 823 2d av
Puthuff Mary, milliner, res 1027 3d av
Puthuff Mrs. Mary, res s s 3d av, West Huntington
PUTHUFF & TERRELL, (Miss J. M. P. & Mrs. C. H. T.), milliners, 1027 3d av
Puthuff Thomas, res 823 2d av

Q

Quarles Charles, machine hand, bds 1941 6th av
Quarles Mrs. Jennie, col'd, res 751 3d av
Quarles Thomas, col'd, laborer, res 751 3d av
Quinlan M. A. fireman, res 710 6th av
Quinlan M. E. fireman, res 710 6th av
Quinlan John, brakeman, res 710 6th av
Quinlan Mary, res 710 6th av
Quinlan Mrs. Susan, boarding house, res 710 6th av

R

Rader E. C. clerk, res cor 2d av and 9th st
Radford Jennie, col'd, res 2 Buffington Row
Rains Cyrithia, res 1732 8th av
Rains John, painter, res 1732 8th av
Rains J. P. carpenter, res 1732 8th av
Rains Wm. carpenter, res 1732 8th av
Raines Ed. brakeman, res 627 9th st

PUTHUFF & TERRELL,

⋙FASHIONABLE⋙

→MILLINERS,←

------AND DEALERS IN------

ALL KINDS OF NOTIONS

AND MATERIAL FOR FANCY WORK.

HUNTINGTON, W. VA.

Raines Matt T. brukeman, res 927 9th st
Raines Maggie, res 627 9th st
Raines Susie, res 627 9th st
Raines W. L. carpenter, res 627 9th st
Raines Walter, freight conductor, res 627 9th st
Ramsey Mrs. E. R. music teacher, res 1248 4th av
Ramsey Lelia O. res 1248 4th av
Ramsey R. C. telegraph operator, res 1248 4th av
Ramsey Dr. R. Y. physician and surgeon, res 1248 4th av
Rau & Beal, barbers, 937 3d av
Rau John, barber, 937 9th st, res 842 and 844 5th av
Randolph Mrs. Lub, col'd, res 747 s s 2d av b7th and 8th sts
Randolph Nelson, col'd, waiter, res 747 s s 2d av b 7th and
    8th sts
Rapold Adam, butcher, 1053 3d av, res 1015½ 3d av
Rapold Katie, res 1015½ 3d av
Rardin Mrs. M. E. res 525 9th st
Ratliff Belle, res 1102 7th av
Ratliff Mrs. F. E. res 8th st b 2d and 3d av

G. F. RATLIFF,

FAMILY GROCERY,

Cor. 7th Ave. and 9th Street.

HUNTINGTON, W. VA.

RATLIFF G. F. attorney-at-law and merchant, 902 and 904 7th av, res 1132 6th av
Ratliff Mrs. Jennie, res 1132 7th av
Ratliff J. F. operator, res 1132 7th av
Ratliff Susan, res 1906 5th av
Ratliff Mrs. S. H. res 8th st b 2d and 3d avs
RATLIFF M. B. restaurant and groceries, 212 9th st
Ratliff Mrs. N. A. res 1134 6th av
Ray B. F. core maker, res 1848 5th av
Ray D. B. core maker, res 1848 5th av
Ray Mrs. Emma, seamstress, res 903 2d av
Ray Emma, res 1848 5th av
Ray, Ed. T. laborer, res 1848 5th av
Ray James, locomotive engineer, res 1021 7th av
Rayburn Dona, 1342 3d av
Ransberry Robert, col'd, porter, 7th av hotel
Realy George, porter, res 629 9th av
Reamer Joseph, painter, bds 1007 3d av
Rece Dora, res 519 13th st
Rece Jennie, school teacher, bds 1242 3d av
Rece Edward, helper, bds 1031 6th av
Rece Frank, bank clerk, res 529 12th st
Rece H. V. physician, 330 9th st, res 1031 4th av
Rece James R. bds 1031 4th av
Rece Wm. tinner, bds 1033 6th av
Reed C. L. car inspector, res 919 6th av
Reed D. H. Rev. minister, res 1119 6th av
Reed F. E. blacksmith, res 11 Brick Row
Reed George, machinist, res 11 Brick Row
Reed J. M. carpenter, res 1119 6th av
Reed Mary, res 11 Brick Row

JOHN RIEF,

GENERAL

Blacksmithing

AND CARRIAGE WORK.

HORSESHOEING A SPECIALTY.

Ninth Street, bet. Fifth and Sixth Aves.

HUNTINGTON, W. VA.

Reed, Mrs. M. D. res 1119 6th av
Reid A. S. carpenter, bds 901 6th av
Reice Nellie, clerk, res 832 6th av
Reinwald August, carpenter, res 1930 Buffington Row
Reynolds Mrs. D. M. bds 721 3d av
Reynolds Millie, res 1112 4th av
REMMELE C. C. merchant, 803 3d av, res 826 6th av
Remmele C. F. baker, res 826 6th av
Remmele Helen, res 826 6th av
Rhodes Mary, col'd, res 13 Buffington Row
Richards F. H. engineer, res Maple av b 19th and 20th sts
Richards Mary, res 1019 7th av
Richardson Samuel, col'd, servant, res 915 6th av
Richardson W. S. R. F. of E. C. & O. R. R. res 1106 7th av
Richinson Ida, col'd, housework, res 1127 6th av
Richie Frank, laborer, res 1829 4th av
Richey Emma, stenographer, res 516 9th st

Rickabaugh T. A. musical agent, bds 926 6th av .
Ricketts A. V. res 1138 4th av
Ricketts Charles, grocer, 625 10th st, res 1138 4th av
Ricketts G. C. grocer, 1049 and 1051 3d av, res w s 11th
 st b 3d and 4th avs
Ricketts Virginia, res 309 11th st
Rief Edith, res 832 6th av
RIEF JOHN. blacksmith, res 832 6th av; shop in rear
Rief Nellie, res 832 6th av
Rief Minnie, res 832 6th av
Rider J. W. clerk, res 349 4th av
Rider Miss M. F. bookkeeper, res 4th av and 4th sts
Riddle James, laborer, res 1940 College av
Ridenour M. A. carpenter, res 2220 4th av
Riffle John, res 822 7th av
Rigg H. Lee, baker, 825 3d av, res 823 6th av
Rigg John, baker, 825 3d av res 823 6th av
Rile Joseph, carpenter, res 713 3d av
Ripley Amos, wheelwright, res 3d av b 10th and 11th sts
Ritz Mrs. Kate, res 944 4th av
Roach McClellen, car builder. res 1823 3d av
Roach Sherman, carpenter, res 1819 4th av
Roach Wilson W. carpenter, bds 1140 4th av
Roadcap & McGinnis (A. G. R. & F. J. McG.) saloon-
 keepers, 327 9th st, rms same
Roadcap A. G. (R. & McGinnis) saloon-keeper, 327 9th
 st, rms same
Rolfe Augusta L, res 641 5th av
Rolfe Annie R. boarding house, 641 5th av
Rolfe C. R. machinist, res 641 5th av
Rood Clint, laborer, res 2d av b 5th and 6th sts
Rood Elizabeth, res 14th st b 2d and 3d avs
Rood Frank, laborer, res 2d av b 5th and 6th sts
Rood George, peddler, res 2d av b 5th and 6th sts
Rood Henderson, res s s 3d av, West Huntington
Rood John, laborer, res 14th st b 2d and 3d av
Rood J. O. laborer, res s s 3d av, West Huntington
Rood Miss T. res s s 3d av, West Huntington
Roadcap George, conductor, res 706 8th st
Roberts A. W. teamster, bds 1215 3d av
Roberts Gracie, res 8 Buffington Row
Roberts H. B. molder. res 312 21st st
Roberts J. D. car builder, res 1905 5th av
Roberts John, laborer, res 8 Buffington Row

Roberts Sanford, painter, res 29 Buffington Row
Robertson R. T. baggage master, 7th av hotel
Robertson W. E. sawyer, res s s 5th av b 5th and 6th sts
Robey Wm. A. carpenter, res Guyandotte river above railroad bridge
Robison Henry, col'd, laborer, res 731 3d av
Robinson C. L. engineer, res 1114 6th av
Robinson James, col'd, hod carrier, res 729 alley b 3d and 4th avs and 7th and 8th sts.
Robinson James, col'd, porter, res 417 9th st
Robinson J. G. core maker, res 1205 3d av
Robinson Mrs. Maggie, res 729 alley
Robinson Mrs. Matilda, res 1114 6th av
Robinson Mrs. Mary, col'd, res 417 9th st
Robinson Minta A. dressmaker, res 1820 4th av
Robinson Y. M. car builder. res 1736 4th av
Robinson Wash. laborer, res 729 alley b 3d and 4th avs
Robinson Wilbert, laborer, res 1736 4th av
Robinson Wm. carpenter, res 526 8th st
Rock James, res n s 3d av West Huntington
Roe Harry V. blacksmith, res 1703 Virginia av
Roe Ira C. painter, res 1703 Virginia av
Roe Luther M. office boy, res 1703 Virginia av
Rogers L. brick mason, res 1125 4th av
Rogers Phillip, res 1947 Buffington av
Rogers R. B. machinist, res 215 8th st
Rolph Fannie, res 1929 4th av
Rolph Lewis, grocer, res 1939 4th av
Rolph Wm. miller, res 1929 4th av
Rose Bettie, col'd, res 316 11th st
Rose C. E. mail carrier, res 617 3d av
Rose Ed col'd, res 316 11th st
Rose Mrs. Elizabeth, col'd, res 826 8th av
Rose I. B. res 617 3d av
Rose John B. col'd, porter, bds 3d av b 9th and 10th st
Rosensteel H. F. foreman, res 1 Brick Row
Rosensteel Miss I. L. res 1 Brick Row
Rosensteel J. A. brakeman, res 1 Brick Row
Ross George, laborer, res 1815 Virginia av
Ross Mrs. Jane, res 2d av and 3d st
Ross John E. cook, res 733 4th av
Ross James M. carpenter, res 733 4th av
Ross Mary, col'd, res 833 4th av
Ross Maggie, res 733 4th av

Ross Orna, res 733 4th av
Ross Owen, cook, res 733 4th av
Roth Wm. moulder, res 2356 1st av
Rouse Samuel, laborer, res 1854 8th av
Row B. W. railroader, res 314 9th st
Row L. H. railroader, res 314 9th st
ROW W. D. physician, res 314 9th st
Rowe Elizabeth, res 15 Buffington av
Rowlance James E. striker, res 717 20th st
Rowser J. J. teacher, res 1946 College av
Royal Coffee & Spice Co., (H. C. Harvey. H. B. Hagen,
    and Geo. F. Miller, Jr.) Packers of Coffee and Baking
    Powders, 1016 3d av
Rucker Dick, col'd, waiter, res cor 2d av and 8th st
Rumbaugh J. H. car builder, res n 24th st
Runyon George, laborer, res 923 2d av
Russell Henry, janitor, res 919 7th av.
RUSSELL GEN. J. HOOE, Pres. Bank of Hunting-
    ton, bds Florentine hotel
Russell James, clerk, res 919 7th av
Russell Wm. bill poster, res 919 7th av

S

Sadler Lindsey, printer, res 525 10th st
SADLER, MARTIN & CO., publishers Baptist Ban-
    ner, 930½ 4th st
Sadler Rev. R. R. (S., Martin & Co.) editor of Banner, res.
    525 10th st
Salmon E. A. Deputy Clerk County Court, bds 1015 6th av
Salmon J. M. boiler maker, res 2261 8th av
Sameth Wm. merchant, n 24th st, res Guyandotte
Sample Mrs. M. E. res 922 4th av
Sampson Mrs. Emily, res 1137 6th av
Sampson George E. traveling engineer, res 1231 5th av
Samuels Col. J. S. clerk, res 1844 5th av
Sanborn L. D. liveryman, 308 and 312 12th st, res 1201 3d
    av
Sanborn M. E. res 1201 3d av
Sanborn Wm. clerk, bds 804 4th av
Sands Jenkie V. clerk, res 623 3d av
Sands Wm. iron roofer, res 623 3d av
Sanders Amanda, res 1823 8th av
Sanders A. H. traveling salesman, res 1314 4th av

Sanders G. W. carpenter, res 733 3d av
Sanders George W. grocer, res 1823 8th av
Sanders H. M. carpenter, res 1908 4th av
Sanders James F. blacksmith, res 1823 8th av
Sanders Mattie, res 6th av b 13th and 14th sts
Sander Mary E. res 1314 4th av
Sanders S. D. res 1847 8th av
Sandman Mrs. Annie, grocery, 717 2d av s s, res same
Sandman Clara, clerk, res 819 2d av s s
Sandman George, shoemaker, res 2d av b 8th and 9th sts
Sanford L. M. clerk, res 913 5th av
Sanford M. R. clerk, w 6th av b 11th and 12th sts
Sanford V. E. car builder, res 1915 Maple av
Sarver G. H. laborer, res 4 Brick Row
Sarver Samuel, res 4 Brick Row
Sarver W. L. laborer, res 4 Brick Row
Saunders C. B. painter, res 1037 7th av
Saunders Emma Miss, col'd, cook, 7th av Hotel
Saunders Dr. E. T. (S. & McCoy), physician and surgeon,
    res 825 5th av
Saunders Robert, laborer, bds 101 24th st
SAYRE JOHN S. photographer, 1007 4th av, res 3d
    av b 11th and 12th sts
Scales Albert, bar tender, rms Continental Hotel
Scales Bros. saloonist, res cor 8th st and 2d av
Scales Henry, res 1913 Buffington av
Scales Peter, res 1949 Buffington av
Scanlon Jennie V. Mrs. res 1144 4th av
Scanlon Maurice, molder. res 1835 4th av
Scanlon Patrick, agent of Mrs. L. G. Bullington, rms 1222
    3d av
Scanlon T. S. shoe dealer, 956 3d av, res 1144 4th av
Schafer Emma Miss, col'd. res 1954 6th av
Schaffer Grant, molder, Ensign Wks, res 101 24th st
Schaefer J. C., salesman, res Alderson, W. Va.
Schlemmer Jacob, baker, 840 3d av, res same
Schmauch Henry, tailor, 813 3d av, res same
Schmauch Louisa, 813 3d av
Schoenfeld Max cigar maker, 717 3d av b
Schoultz Chas. laborer, res 1742 College av
Schreiber Charles, res 1411 4th av
Schreiber Louis, wks Martin's mill, res 1411 4th av
Schreiber Wm. wks Martin's mill, res 1411 4th av

JOHN S. SAYRE

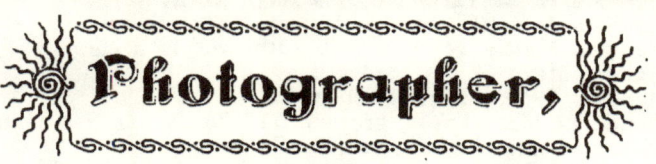

Photographer,

No. 1007 FOURTH AVENUE,   Near Tenth Street,

Makes a Specialty of Fine Portraits of all Sizes. Old Pictures Copied, Enlarged and Finished in Crayon, India Ink, Water Colors or Oil Colors.

All work guaranteed satisfactory, and done at the very lowest price possible.

Views of Business Houses, Private Residences, Family Groups, Lawn Parties, Etc. attended to on short notice.

Schultz Sherman, tinner, 1033 3d av, res West Huntington
Schump John, brakeman, bds 523 10th st
Schwable Cassie Miss, gilder, 927 2d av, res West Huntington
Scott Abner, col'd, laborer, bds 213 8th st b 2d and 3d
Scott Carrie, helper, res 941 3d av
Scott Edward, col'd, hod carrier, bds 1208 3d av alley
Scott George, col'd, watchman, bds 751 3d av
Scott Isham, fireman, Ensign Co., res 320 8th av
Scott John W. col'd, res 820 8th av
Scott Mabelle Miss, first assistant teacher, Marshall College. the State Normal School, bds Marshall College
Scott Paul, teacher, bds 1013 6th av
Scott Scott, hod carrier, res 1208 3d av alley
Seals Charles L. barber. bds 3d av b 8th and 9th sts
Seamands G. Miss, res 1820 8th av
Seamands P. H. lineman, res 1820 8th av
Seamands R. M. brakeman. res 1513 R. R. b 15th and 16th
Sears Gussie M. Miss, res 936 4th av

SEVENTH AVENUE HOTEL,

Cor. Seventh Ave. and Ninth St.

NEW BUILDING AND NEW FURNITURE!

BEST MEALS FOR THE LEAST MONEY!

Situated Near Passenger Depot.

A. D. TAYLOR,
PROPRIETOR.

J. A. TAYLOR,
MANAGER.

Sebastian George W. conductor C. & O. res 1209 3d av
Sedgwick E. res 1956 4th av
Sedgwick Frank, laborer, Ensign Co. res 1956 4th av
Seegmiller Ludwig, helper, Ensign Wks, res N 24th st
Seegmiller Peter, molder, Ensign Wks, res N 24th st
Sensney Jacob N. foreman. Ensign Wks, res 1753 3d av
Sensney Susie E. Miss, res 1753 3d av
SEVENTH AVENUE HOTEL, 838 7th av
Sexton Cowan, col'd, laborer, res 1315 18th st
Seybert J. S. car builder, Ensign Wks bds 315 11th st
Shackelford John, grocery-man, bds 844 3d av
Shanallian Pat, tailor, bds 416 8th st
SHANK T. M. Excelsior Mattress Factory, 2d av & 14th
Shanks J. Mell, machinist, 1012 6th av
Shanley Pat, tailor, bds e s 8th st b 4th and 5th av
Sharitz C. J. farmer, res 1907 3d av.
Sharitz Seldon N. fireman, res 1907 5th av
Sharp Victoria, col'd, servant, 1321 3d av
Shaver Henry F. carpenter, res 10 Frame Row
Shaver John, col'd, res 12 West Buffington Row
Shaw Claude, carpenter, res 631 3d av
Shaw Edna Miss, costume maker, res 631 3d av
Shaw Emma Miss, dressmaker, res 631 3d av
Shaw J. C. boarding house, res 631 3d av
Shaw L. C. postal clerk, res 1125 4th av
Sheets & Myers, merchants, 827 3d av, s e cor 11th st
  and 6th av
Shields Allie M. Miss, col'd, ironer, res 727 Alley, b 2d
  and 3d and 7th and 8th sts
Shields James, col'd, waiter, res 406 9th st

Shields James, col'd, wks at Florentine Hotel, res 822 7th
    av alley
Shelton Ellen, Mrs. col'd, laundress, res 727 Alley b 2d
    and 3d and 7th and 8th
Shelton James H. civil engineer, res 1208 7th av
Shelton J. R. speculator, res 1207 5th av
Shelton Mary Y. res 1208 7th av
Shelton Miss Stella M. res 1208 7th av
Shelton Thos. carpenter, res 909 7th av
Shelton Walter T. railroad engineer, res 1208 7th av
Shelton W. E. laborer, res 1948 8th av
Shepherd Miss Grace, res 817 6th av
Shepherd Mrs. Margaret, res 817 6th av
Sheppard Mollie, laundress, Continental Hotel
Shepherd T. R. attorney, P. O. building, 328½ 9th st
Sheff J. C. carpenter, bds cor 8th st and 2d av
SHIFFLETTE J. L. news dealer, 401 9th st, res St.
    Nicholas Hotel.
Shively Miss Emma, cook, res 1131 6th av
Shiveley John, cutter, res 914 Fourth av
Shore George L. carpenter, res s e cor 5th av and 8th st
SHORE E. agent, contractor and builder, 913 4th av,
    res s e cor 5th av and 8th st
Shore William, carpenter, 913 4th av, res 6th av b 7th and
    8th st
Shoemaker Elizabeth, res North 24th st
Shoemaker J. H. molder, Ensign Wks, res North 24th st
Shoemaker L. D. machinist, bds 641 5th av
Shumaker Lee, molder, Ensign Wks, res 1943 Buffington
    av
Shumate Wm. laborer, res 4 Burk's Row
Shy Alvio, timekeeper, bds 1931 Buffington av
Shy Emma, res 14th st nr 11th av
Shy Frank, laborer, Ensign Wks, res 2217 3d av
Shy Coll. res s s 3d av, West Huntington
Shy W. E. res 14th nr 11th av
Shyer Celia, res 954 3d av
Shyer S. clothing and dry goods, 954 3d av, res same
Shyer S. Jr. clerk, 954 3d av
Sidney Bettie, col'd, laundress, res n s alley, b 8th and
    9th st
Sidney Bettie, laundress, res 406 9th st
Sidney Ella, laundress, res 406 9th st
Simms George, res 2405 2d av

ELIZABETH SHORE,

CONTRACTOR

AND BUILDER.

——DEALER IN——

FLOORING, WEATHER-BOARDING and DRESSED LUMBER.

Planing, Scroll Sawing & Turning

DONE TO ORDER.

All kinds of LUMBER SAWED on Short Notice.

MILL, SOUTH SIDE FOURTH AVE.

Between Ninth and Tenth Streets,

HUNTINGTON, W. VA.

112   HUNTINGTON [SLO] DIRECTORY.

SIMMS & ENSLOW (H. C. S. & F. B. E.), attorneys-at-law, 222 10th st
Simms Fannie, res 2405 2d av
Simms Frank, teamster, res 1920 Locust av
Simms H. C. (S. & Enslow), attorney-at-law, 222 10th st, res 1137 3d av
Simms Kate F. Mrs. res 1137 3d av
Simms Lavenia, res 2405 2d av
Simms Lida, res 2405 2d av
Simms Sarah, res 2405 2d av
Simms Wm. laborer, res 2405 2d av
Sims Bettie, res 731 Alley, b 7th and 8th sts and 4th and 5th av
Sims Florence, col'd, cook, res 529 12th st
Simon Kate Mrs. res 908 7th av
Simons H. L. minister, res 1438 3d av
Simons Laura B. res 814 4th av
Simons Mrs Matilda, res 814 4th av
Simons Mary Jane, res 814 4th av
Simons W. M. res 814 4th av
Simmons Eugenia, col'd, res 116 24th st
Simmons Fannie, res 1011 5th av
Simmons Lizzie, 1011 5th av
Simmons Martin, confectioner, 416 9th st, res 4th av b 8th and 9th st
Simmons W. H. machinist, res 1140 4th av
Simmons W. M. clerk, res 904 4th av b 8th and 9th sts
Simpson J. B. shoemaker, bds 804 4th av
SIMPSON WM. justice of the peace, 910 3d av, res 804 4th av
SINGER MFG. CO. 1042 3d av, W. T. Brockmeyer, mgr
Sink Fred, baker, 328 9th st, bds 1015 6th av
Sinsel Estelle, res 1136 3d av
Sinsel Maud, res 1136 3d av
Sites B. F. carpenter, res 1125 4th av
Skeens Mary, res 916 5th av
Skeenes Polly, res 1031 4th av
Skeer Thos. J. molder, Ensign Wks, res 1554 3d av
Skelton Annie V. teacher, res 1137 3d av
Slaughter James, bottler, s s 2d av b 9th and 10th sts, bds 731 2d av b 7th and 8th sts
SLOAN REV. J. M. pastor First Presbyterian Church, res 1019 5th av

Sloan Mrs. J. M. res 1019 5th av
Smith A. G. fireman, res 1413 8th av on railroad
Smith A. M. brakeman, res 1413 8th av on alley
Smith Aaron, brakeman, res 739 4th av
Smith Albert, col'd, cook, res 4th av b 8th and 9th sts
Smith Allen, pattern maker, Ensign Wks, res 1901 Virginia av
Smith Ambrose, laborer, res 1854 8th av
Smith Mrs. Annetta, res 621 12th st
Smith Bertha, res 703 5th av
Smith Bettie, bds 322 18th st
Smith B. E. molder, Ensign Wks, res 503 20th st
Smith B. H. laborer, res 1926 Maple av
Smith Clara B. res 1227 6th av
Smith D. B. engineer, res 1126 7th av
Smith D. M. bartender, res 1121 4th av
Smith E B. res Saints' Rest
Smith Ellison, machinist, Ensign Wks, bds 2145 3d av
Smith Eliza Mrs. res 1141 3d av
Smith Fanny, col'd, res 531 W. 9th st
Smith Frank, shoemaker, 752 3d av b 7th and 8th sts, res
    n s Alley b 4th and 5th avs and 7th and 8th sts
SMITH G. W. restaurant, 837 3d av, res 3d av
Smith G. W. machinist, res 1227 6th av
Smith G. W. well digger, res 1843 Virginia av
Smith Mrs. Hannah, res 4th av b 13th and 14 sts
Smith Harry, carpenter, res 739 alley b 7th and 8th sts
    and 4th and 5th avs
Smith Henry T. engineer, rms 1032 7th av
Smith Henry, col'd, shoemaker, res 621 9th st
Smith Inez, res 1023 6th av
Smith Jas. C. teamster, Gordon's saw mill, res 1632 2d av
Smith J. L. brakeman, res 1413 8th av
Smith J. R. machinist, Ensign Co. res 2425 1st av
Smith J. W. driver, res 1046 3d av
Smith Jacob, tinner, res s s 3d av, West Huntington
Smith Jackson, teamster, res 1848 4th av
Smith James, molder, res n 24th st
Smith Jos. boiler maker, bds 1926 Maple av
Smith John, carpenter, res 1824 8th av
Smith Sada, res 1824 8th av
Smith Laura, res 1824 8th av
Smith Lenna V. res 1854 4th av
Smith M. E. grocer, 655 3d av, res Saints' Rest

Best Kanawha and Ohio River COAL,

At Coal Yard, near Passenger Depot,
Cor. 8th Ave. & 8th St.   THOS. MEDFOR' Prop.

Smith Mallissa, res 828 3d av
Smith Mahala B. res 1632 2d av
Smith Mrs. Mattie, tailoress, 221 9th st, res same
Smith N. clerk, res 1141 3d av
Smith Nap. col'd, porter, rms 835 2d av
Smith Obediah, laborer, res 1236 4th alley
Smith Mrs. Patrick, res 805 7th av
Smith R. teamster, res cor 14th st and 13th av
Smith Thomas, res n 24th st
Smith W. B. tailoring, 221 9th st res same
Smith W. E. druggist, 2001 3d av, res same
Smith W. H. tinner, res Saints Rest
Smith William, res 731 alley b 7th and 8th sts and 4th
      and 5th avs
Smith Winslow, car builder, res 1854 4th av
Smoot J. W. carpenter, res 1920 Maple av
Snedegar A. A. engineer, res 924 7th av
Snedegar Maggie B. res 655 3d av
Snedegar Robert, engineer, res 1123 6th av
SNIDER BROTHERS (Charles, Joseph and Fre-
      mont S.); bakers and confectioners, 1005 3d av
Snider Charles, (S. Bros.) baker, bds 1007 3d av
Snider Fremont, (S. Bros.), baker, res 1112 4th av
Snider G. W. painter, res 1118 4th av
Snider Joseph, (S. Bros.), baker, rms 729 6th av
Snider Martin, car builder, res 1844 8th av
Snider Mrs. Mattie E. res 1112 4th av
Snider William, fireman, res 655 3d av
Snell Cora, res 101 24th st
Snoddy Mary, domestic, res 1037 3d av
Snowberger Charley, moulder, res 2405 2d av
Snyder Mrs. Paulina, boarding house, 847 4th av
Sole Mrs. Delaware, res 1145 3d av
Solman J. K. clerk and notary public, 428 Court House,
      res Barboursville
Solomon Saunders, head engineer, res 8th av b 18th and
      19th sts
Songer Edward, axle maker, res n 24th st
Songer James B. laborer, res n 24th st
Songer G. W. axle maker, res n 24th st
Songer Miss L. B. res n 24th st
Sours Anna, res 1049 4th av
Sours William, painter, res 1048 4th av
Southards Arzilia, servant, res 1016 4th av

Southern News Co. and Dining Room, C. & O. depot
Southworth Andrew, 1008 6th av
Southworth A. F. engineer, res 1008 6th av
Southworth C. J. res 1008 6th av
Southworth Nettie, res 1008 6th av
Spafford A. T. assistant yard master, res 1218 6th av
Spafford C. E. carpenter, res 1218 6th av
SPANGENBERG & CO. (H. Spangenberg & Co.) mnfrs. of cigars and dealers in smokers' articles, 927 3d av, res 930 6th av
Sparks Charles, laborer, res 937 4th alley
Spears Ella, res 733 6th av
Spears Jennie, res 733 6th av
SPENCE G. L. music and art establishment, 911 3d av
Spencer Annie C. res 1356 3d av
Spencer Frank, showman, Bon Ton Theater 8th and 9th sts
Spencer Mrs. Fannie W. res 1356 3d av
Spencer Susan, res 2d av b 8th and 9th sts
Spencer T. Roy, res 1356 3d cor 14th st
Spickard E. L. molder, Ensign Co. res 2435 1st av
Spiller L. C. car builder, Ensign Co. res 1739 4th av
Sprinkles Earnest, laborer, Ensign Co. res 1903 8th av
Sprinkles Edward, tinner, res 1903 8th av
Sproul Charles, col'd, laborer, Ensign Co. res 1948 Maple av
Spurlock Geo. laborer, res 4 Brick Row
Spurlock Jesse, car builder, Ensign Co. res 2225 3d av
St. Clair Effie, rms 313 11th st
ST. CHARLES HOTEL (New), W. W. Herring, prop. 901 6th av
St. Nicholas Hotel, Alf. M. Thompson, prop. 939-41-41½ 3d av
Staley A. J. policeman, res 1916 6th av
Staley Andrew, conductor, res 529 12th st
Staley C. E. carpenter, res 1933 6th av
Staley Jeneva, res 1933 6th av
Staley Jos. foreman, Ensign Co. res 1933 6th av
Staley W. O. M. car finisher, Ensign Co, res 1936 6th av
Staley Oscar R. photographer, res 1939 6th av
Staley Olive S. res 1939 6th av
Staley Solomon, laborer, res 4 Buffington Row
Stafford N. painter, Ensign Co. res 2231 3d av
Stanley B K. wheel molder, Ensign Co. res 2419 1st av

Stanley Blanche. res 2419 1st av
Stanley H. J. brakeman, res 1120 7th av
Stanley James, res 623 3d av
Stanley May. res 2419 1st av
Stanley Wm. car builder, Ensign Co. res 1947 8th av
Starck Geo. laborer, Ensign Co. bds 1815 Virginia av
Starck Jno. laborer. Ensign Co. res 1815 Virginia av
Starkey John, machinist, res Love Block
Starkey Wm. carpenter, res b 2d and 3d avs on 8th st
Starkey Wm. teamster, res Love Block
Staten Mary C. Mrs. teacher, res 948 3d av
Stead Sam, shoemaker, 752 3d av
Stead Sarah, res 752 3d av
Steagall M. J. res 1415 Railroad
Stephens J. A. carpenter, res 1936 Buffington av
Stephens T. C. baggage master, res 1405 8th av alley
Stephenson Ella, res 1032 7th av
Stephenson Eliza, res 1032 7th av
Stephenson Emma Mrs. res 1905 8th av
Stephenson Etta Mrs. res 812 6th av
Stephenson J. A. carpenter, bds cor 8th st and 2d av
Stephenson Jennie Mrs. res 828 3d av
Stephenson H. D. carpenter. res 1932 Buffington av
Stephenson M. A. res 828 3d av
Stephenson H. carpenter, res 1032 7th av
Stephenson Lena, res 1032 7th av
Stephenson R P. res 1695 8th av
Stephenson V. W. bartender, b 916 5th av
Sterling S. R. clerk, Ensign Co. res 1749 3d av
Sternberger L. saloon keeper, 1009 3d av, res 1037 4th av
Stevens Jane. res 1014 6th av alley
Stevens Harvey, tinner, bds 2335 8th av
Stevens C. painter, Ensign Co. res 1811 Virginia av
Stevens Vincent, painter, Ensign Co, res 1847 Virginia av
Stevens Wm. painter, Ensign Co. res 1738 5th av
Stevenson Philip, laborer, res 3d av b 8th and 9th sts
Stewart Ada M. res 1663 8th av
Stewart B H. laborer, res s s 3d av, West Huntington
Stewart C. B. res 1663 8th av
Stewart Claud L. res 1663 8th av
Stewart C. S. clerk, bds 734 3d av
Stewart H. D. clerk, res 734 3d av
Stewart H. F. painter, bds 734 3d pv
Stewart I. F. deputy sheriff, res 1663 8th av

JAMES B. STEWART,
ARCHITECT,

— WILL MAKE —

Plans and Specifications

For all kinds of Buildings, and will superintend the construction of the same.

WILL ALSO MAKE ALL

KINDS OF MECHANICAL DRAWINGS

— FOR —

Construction and for Patent Office Models.

OFFICE: above Millender & Bierman's Planing Mill,

THIRD AV., HUNTINGTON, W. VA.

STEWART JAS. B. architect, 1120 3d av
Stewart J. B. baggage master, res 927 7th av
Stewart J. S. street commissioner
Stewart Kenley, col'd, drayman, res 729 alley b 6th and 7th avs
Stewart Lulu, assistant teacher at Marshall College (the State Normal School), bds Marshall College
Stewart Mary A. res s s 3d av, West Huntington
Stewart Nancy, res s s 3d av, West Huntington
Stewart Mrs. S. A. res 1321 3d av
Still Chas. core maker, Ensign Co. res n 24th st
Stockham C. P. blacksmith, res 1715 8th av
Stockton Mrs. res 406 9th st
Stokes Jennie, res 1119 4th av alley
Stokes Mrs. M. res 751 3d av
Stone Lela F. res 2d av b 8th and 9th sts
Stone Lizzie, boarding house, 313 11th st
Stone O. M. salesman, res 1906 5th av
Stone O. M. phrenologist, res 2d av b 8th and 9th
Stormes H. G. carpenter, res 731 4th av

Stout T. E. attorney, 910 3d av
STOUT & KING, attorneys, 910 3d av
Strange J. R. baggage master, res 808 6th av
Strange W. H. brakeman, bds 808 6th av
Stratton C. G. baggage master, res 920 7th av
Strong T. painter, res 828 7th av alley
Strother Sophia Mrs. bds 225 24th st
Strother W. R. brick mason, bds 1316 4th av
Strow Henry, machinist, res 1938 Locust av
Strow James, machinist, res 1938 Locust av
Strow Miriam, res 1938 Locust av
Studrick John, col'd, res 834 7th av alley
Sturgeon J. W. machinist, res 1615 2d av
Succo Jennie, res 420 19th st
Suckert C. conductor, bds 1016 6th av
Sullivan Alonzo, laborer, res 1732 5th av
Sullivan L. C. res 1732 College av
Sullivan Sarah M. res 1732 College av
Sullivan Alvin, res 1935 4th av
Sullivan Fannie, res 1953 4th av
Sullivan Henry, farmer, res 1953 4th av
Sullivan Maggie, res 1953 4th av
Sullivan Wm. res 1953 4th av
Summers M. J. baggage master, res 519 13th st
Summers W. H. res 747 4th av
Summers Vernie, res 747 4th av
Sutphin James S. sup't ice factory, res 815 6th av
SWAIN J. C. city assessor, res 529 12th st
Swain Albert, telegrapher, bds 1218 4th av
Swan Eliza, res 13 Buffington Row
Swan J. W. watchman, res 13 Buffington Row
Swan Oliver, laborer, res 13 Buffington Row
Swan W. E. printer, res 1125 4th av
Swann F. B. printer, bds 4th av
Sylvis G. D. machinist, 1102 7th av

T

Tabor Mary Mrs. dressmaker, res 1915 Maple av
Tailor Bettie, res 1686 8th av
Tailor Geo. res 1 Buffington Row
Tailor H. C. brakeman, res 1686 8th av
Tailor John, col'd, res 1 Beardsley Row

Tailor Mary, res 1 Buffington Row
Taliaferro C. E. machinist, res 1008 4th av
Taliaferro L. H. bartender, res 1008 4th av
Talifaro Louis, barkeeper, rms 219 10th st
Tallman W. A. prop Merchants' Hotel, cor 2d av and 9th
 st
Tanner Emma Mrs. res 1047 4th av
Tanner J. C. machinist, res 1047 4th av
Tate John, laborer, res 414 9th st
Tate Lee, salesman, res cor 6th av and 10th st
Tate Minnie, res 414 9th st
Tate Wesly, res 414 9th st
Taylor A. B. machinist, res 1925 6th av
Taylor A. D. prop 7th Av Hotel, 838 7th av
Taylor A. D. saloon keeper, 535 9th st, res 639 9th st
Taylor C. Truehart, res s s 3d av, West Huntington
Taylor J. A. hotel manager, 838 7th av
Taylor J. B. machinist, res 1102 7th av
Taylor Mattie F. res s s 3d av, West Huntington
Taylor Mary Mrs. res 216 12th st
Taylor Maud, res 833 7th av
Taylor Richard, drayman, res 1046 3d av
Taylor S. F. Mrs. res 833 7th av
TAYLOR T. W. justice of the peace, 904½ 3d av. res
 Central City
Teice Lewis, tinner, 1033 3d av, res 541 10th st
Temple O. G. engineer, res 1013 7th av
Terrell C. H. machinist, res 1013 6th av
Terrell C. H. Mrs. (Puthoff & T.), milliner, 1027 3d av,
 res s s 6th av b 10th and 11th sts
Terwilliger Oscar, pool tables, bds 753 and 755 8th st
Terry Annie Mrs. seamstress, bds 1215 3d av
Terry J. Russell, fresco painter, res cor 4th av and 13th st
Terry Viola, res cor 13th and 4th av
Testament J. J. machinist, res 426 17th st
Teubert J. W. merchant, 801 7th av, res 803 7th av
Thacker Kate, servant, res 1047 4th av
Thackston B. H. judge county court, res 1655 8th av
Thackston Charles C. clerk, res 1655 8th av
Thackston Eugenia, res 1655 8th av
Thackston James A. brakeman, res 1655 8th av
Thackston Kate C. res 1655 8th av
Thackston Lida F. res 1655 8th av
Thackston Sally C. res 1655 8th av

Thackston W. M. fireman, res 1655 8 av
Tharp Geo. carpenter, res 1131 4th av
Thomas A. C. private secretary, Ensign Co. res 1220 6th av
Thomas Chas. E. printer, cor 9th st and 4th av, res 1135 4th av
Thomas Clara E. res 1135 4th av
Thomas F. M. Mrs. music teacher, res 1102 7th av
Thomas Harry, compositor, bds cor 4th and 12th sts
Thomas Harry L. printer, res 1135 4th av
Thomas Joseph, hostler, bds 1212 4th av alley
Thomas John L. barber, res 1943 3d av
Thomas M. C. Miss, res 816 7th av
Thomas M. M. Miss, res 1102 7th av
Thomas Thomas. carpenter, bds 4th av b 13th and 14th st
Thomason Jas. O. laborer, res 1936 6th av
Thomason G. W. painter and carpenter, res 1907 4th av
Thomison E molder, bds n 24th st
Thompson Amos, res 1913 Virginia av
Thompson Alf. M. prop St. Nicholas Hotel, 933, 941 and 941½ 3d av
Thompson A. T. steward, passenger depot
Thompson Chas. laborer, res 1905 Virginia av
Thompson C. E. painter, res 819 7th av
Thompson C. L. res 1216 6th av
Thompson Mrs. E. res 1844 8th av
Thompson E. R. waiter, res cor 2d av and 8th st
Thompson Helen, res 220 12th st
Thompson Jos. E. machinist, res 1913 Virginia av
Thompson J. E. painter, res 819 7th av
Thompson Jas. E. bartender, bds 1922 4th av
Thompson J. M. car builder, res 1815 4th av
Thompson J. T. machinist, res 1712 4th av
Thompson Lucy Mrs. res 1st av and 29th st
Thompson Sarah, res Beardsley Row
Thompson W. H. car builder, res 1811 4th av
Thompson Hon. W. T. State Treasurer, 1st av and 29th sts
Thornburg C. M. fireman, res 813 7th av
Thornburg Thos. Q. brick maker, res 4th av, West Huntington
Thornley Wickham, machinist, res 3d av b 6th and 7th sts
Thornton M. L. timber inspector, res 614 9th st
Throckmorton Mrs. Ella, res 817 4th av alley

Throckmorton Maud, res 817 4th av alley
Thuma Gertie, res 1109 4th av
Thuma John, salesman, res 825 6th av
Thuma Leonard, molder, res 1109 4th av
Thuma O. S. molder, res 4th av b 13th and 14th sts
Thuma T. J. furniture dealer, res 1109 4th av
Thurnley Willis. machinist, bds 631 3d av
Tiernan Wm. M. machinist, res 5th av b 11th and 12th
    sts
Tillinghast D. grocer, res 1908 Buffington av
Tillinghast Dela, res 1908 Buffington av
Tillinghast Geo. grocer, 1912 Buffington av, b 1908 Buf-
    fington av
Tillinghast Wayne, laborer, res 1908 Buffington av
Timberlake David, laborer, res 1946 6th av
Tinsley Lena, res 1727 8th av
Tinsley Mattie Mrs. res 1937 8th av
Tinsley Wm. H. brakeman, res 1727 8th av
Tipton J. A. carpenter, res 1744 8th av
Titus Ivor, foreman molding dept. res 617 9th st
Tolbot Haley, salesman, res 818 7th av
Toney Albert, laborer, res 1856 8th av
Toney G. W. Mrs. res 1047 4th av
Toney Mary, res 1856 8th av
Toney M. N. canvasser, res 1856 8th av
Toney Wm. molder, res 1856 8th av
Toney Theodore, laborer, res 1952 7th av
Toppens Wm. carpenter, bds 916 5th av
Torstein Mary, res 847 4th av
Towberman E. T. lumber inspector, res 1517 3d av
Towery A. C. clerk, res 941 3d av
Trent E. T. clerk, res s e cor 10th st and 3d av
Trice A. J. real estate agent and auctioneer, res s s 5th
    av b 5th and 6th sts
Trice Cora Lee, teacher, res s s 5th av b 5th and 6th sts
Trice Henry A. carpenter, res s s 5th av b 5th and 6th
    sts
Trice Susie, cook, res 7th Av Hotel
Trimmer Ada P. res 1729 3d av
Trimmer T. L. core maker, res 1729 3d av
True John, yard master, res 1826 8th av
Trumbo R. L. car builder, res 1209 3d av
Tubert J. H. grocer, res 801 7th av
Tucker C. C. janitor at Marshall College

Tucker Elias, driver, res 8th av b 16th and 17th sts
TUCKER FRANK, city editor of Herald, 308 10th
    st, res 4th av b 12th and 13th sts
Tucker Hugh G. clerk, res 941 3d av
Turney R. W. foreman, res 1036 6th av
Tuning J. P. teamster, res 1904 4th av
Turley Alex. carpenter, bds 8 Frame Row
TURLEY BROS. Carriage and House Painters, 215
    11th st
Turley Jas. M carpenter, res 1836 8th av
Turley Lee, carpenter, bds 8 Frame Row
Turley Mollie, regalia maker, 1029 and 1031 3d av, res
    1123 6th av
Turley Thomas, carriage and house painter and paper
    hanger, 215 11th st, res Central City
Turley William, carriage and house painter and paper
    hanger, 215 11th st, res Central City
Turner Christopher, col'd, laborer, res 751 3d av
Turner C. W. conductor, res 1419 railroad
Turner David, res 1020 4th av
Turner Eliza Mrs. col'd, res 812 7th av alley
Turner Florence, compositor, res 1020 4th av
Turner James, carpenter, res 1020 4th av
Turner Jerry, agent, rms 753 and 755 8th st
Turner Lizzie, res 1020 4th av
Turner Scott, policeman, rms 217 10th st
Turner Wm. miller, res 817 av alley
Tuttle Scott, wks planing mill, res 1343 4th av
Tylor Julia, nurse, res 1128 3d av
Tylor Mary Mrs. col'd, cook, res 1141 3d av
Tyler P. A. barber, bds cor 20th st and Maple av
Tyree H. F. clerk, bds 823 6th av
Tyree Lizzie, col'd, washing, res 1212 4th av alley
Tyree William, foundryman, res 1212 4th av alley

U

Underwood Enoch, carpenter, res 1936 Locust av
Underwood Francis E. boarding house, res 808 4th av
Union News Co., C. G. Burns, prop. pass depot, res 605
    9th st
Unseld S. J. Mrs. millinery and notions, 1015 3d av, res
    1243 3d av

TURLEY BROTHERS

HOUSE PAINTERS

SIGNS

A SPECIALTY.

GRAINING & CARRIAGE PAINTING

OFFICE AND SHOP:

No. 213 Eleventh Street,

HUNTINGTON, W. VA.

V

Valentine J. W. merchant, 946½ 3d av, res 6th av b 9th
and 10th sts
Vance Henry, molder, res 1744 College av
Vandiver J. H. res 313 11th st
Vandiver Richard, res 313 11th st
Vanfleet A. L. painter, res 1722 8th av
Vanfleet George, carpenter, res 20 Frame Row
Vanhorn Ary, res 1691 8th av
Vanhorn C. H. res 1691 8th av
Vanhorn F. Miss, res 1691 8th av
Vanhorn Gertie Miss, 1691 8th av
Vanhorn M. N. fireman, res 1691 8th av
Vanhorn S. R. carpenter, res 1691 8th av
Van Vleck E. C. dentist, res 511 10th st
Vaugn Emily, res alley b 3d and 4th av and 11th and 12th
sts
Vaughn Harris, col'd, laborer, res alley b 4th and 5th avs
and 11th and 12th sts
Vaughn H. carpenter, res 1223 6th av
Verlander Jas. E. res n s 3d av, West Huntington
Verlander Jno. P. telegrapher, res West Huntington
Vernat Geo. painter, res 22 Buffington Row
Vernat Hudson, painter, res 22 Buffington Row
Vernat Jackson, blacksmith, res 22 Buffington Row
Vernat Judson, laborer, res 22 Buffington Row
Vernat Robt. laborer, res 28 Buffington Row
Vernat Wm. blacksmith, 28 Buffington Row
Via E. F. res 925 3d av
Via H. O. confectioner, 925 3d av
Viars James R. laborer, res 1951 4th av
VICKERS R. E. physician, res 936 3d av
Vickers C. H. carpenter, 412 10th st
**VIENNA BAKERY, CONFECTIONERY and
LUNCH ROOM,** Wm. Waldron, prop. 328 9th st
Vine T. J. wks brickyard, res 1036 7th av
Vines Edna, res 1695 8th av
Vines J. W. laborer, res 1695 8th av
Vines M. C. car inspector, res 1501 s railroad
Vines Mary, res 1501 s railroad
Vines Mattie, res 1501 s railroad
Vinson Chas. C. railroader, res 6th av b 10th and 11th sts
Vinson F. res 1020 6th av

Theory of Music,   Composition,

Thorough Bass,   Arrangement.

Aug. Volkenrath,

❋ TEACHER ✦ OF ✦ MUSIC ❊

N. E. CORNER FOURTH AV. & EIGHTH ST.,   Huntington, W. Va.

Piano,   Banjo,

Organ,   Mandolin,

Violin,   Viola on

Guitar,   Violincello.

Vinson J. A. yard clerk, res 6th av b 10th and 11th sts
Vinson Lulu Maud, res 1020 6th av
VINSON & McDONALD, attorneys, 221½ 10th sts
Vinson Maud L. res 6th av b 10th and 11th sts
Vinson Will, clerk, res 1022 6th av
Vinson Wm. S. clerk, res 6th av b 10th and 11th sts
Vinson Z. T. attorney, res 1239 5th av
VOLKENRATH A. music teacher, res 744 4th av
Volkenrath Agatha, res 744 4th av
Volkenrath Maggie, res 744 4th av

W

Wade Chas. T. laborer, res 1936 Maple av
Wade Jas. K. carpenter, res 1820 4th av
Wagner H. clerk, res 4th av, b 10th and 11th sts
Wagner James, blacksmith, C. & O. res "Patch"
Wagoner Jacob, laborer, res 416 17th st
Wagoner Mary, res 416 17th st
Wakefield Newton, machinist, res 1130 6th av

J. W. McCREADY,

BLACKSMITH and WAGON-MAKER,

Horseshoeing and General Repair Work,

10th St., Between 2d and 3d Aves., Huntington, W. Va.

Waldeck Frank, machinist, res 1116 4th av
Waldron Wm. conductor, res 936 7th av
WALKER CHAS. W. editor Advertiser, 3d av b 8th and 9th sts, rms 5th av
WALKER W. P. D.D. pastor 5th av Baptist Church, res 427 10th st
Walker Eugene, fireman, res 1515 Railroad
Walker Mrs. Eliza, dressmaker, res 622 8th st
Walker E. C. machinist, res 1918 Buffington av
Walker Frank, laborer, res 9 North Ensign shops
Walker Grant, teamster for Millender & Bierman
Walker George W. fireman, res 406 9th st
Walker Harvey, res 1727 4th av
Walker Harvey, machinist, Millender & Bierman's
Walker Henry, waiter, rms 731 3d av
Walker Henry W. teamster, res 1821 Virginia av
Walker Margaret, col'd, res 827 7th av
Walker Richard, teamster, res 1727 4th av
Walkinshaw Jas. A. inspector of weights and measures, res 1001 4th av
Wallace Ella M. compositor, res 936 4th av

WALLACE G. E. publisher Argus, res 936 4th av

Wallace Maud, servant, res s s 5th av b 5th and 6th sts

Wallace Stephen R. feed store, 702, 704 3d av, res 821 6th av

WALLACE W. F. editor Argus, 934 4th av, res 936 4th av

Walter J. L. col'd, bds 1676 8th av

Walton E. F. plasterer, res s s 3d av, West Huntington

Walton G. E. Argus Printing House, 934 4th av

Walton James, baker, res 1117 3d av, West Huntington

Walton Nathaniel, compositor. bds 416 8th st

Walton W. F. Argus Printing House, 934 4th av

Warnick C. D. engineer, bds 1023 6th av

Ward Anna, domestic, res 1035 6th av

Ward C. E. blacksmith, res 830 7th av alley

Ward John, laborer, res 1926 Buffington av

Ward J. E. trace clerk, bds 918 4th av

Ward Peter, book agent, bds cor 8th st and 2d av

Ward Robert C. foreman C. & O. smith shop, res 1214 3d av

Ward Philip, carpenter, res 1914 Locust av

Ware Addie V. res 712 4th av

Ware E. L. cashier Adams Express office, res s e cor 7th av and 10th sts

Ware Frederick A. collector, res 712 4th av

Ware F. H. res 712 4th av

Ware H. H. teacher, res 1005 7th av

Ware Henry, Jr. engineer, res 1105 7th av

Ware Kate B. res 712 4th av

Ware Lee, express messenger, res 1005 7th av

Ware Maria, res 1005 7th av

Ware Susan, res 1005 7th av

Wash Alice C. Mrs. res 940 6th av

Washington Bernard, col'd, res alley b 3d and 4th av and 11th and 12th sts

Washington Charles, hostler, res 941 3d av

Washington Charles, col'd, teamster, 1001 3d av, res Beardsley Row

Washington Fannie, col'd, res alley b 3d and 4th av and 11th and 12th sts

Washington Hannah Mrs. col'd, res 8 Buffington Row

Washington Hedrick, col'd, brakeman, bds 1660 8th av

Washington H. S. timekeeper, bds 1018 6th av

C. L. HOGG,

FEED * STORE.

EVERYTHING IN THE LINE HANDLED,

WHOLESALE AND RETAIL.

— GOOD STOCK OF —

VERY BEST FLOUR

ALWAYS ON HAND AT FAIR PRICES.

→ FIELD ∴ SEEDS ←

A SPECIALTY.

All ∴ Goods ∴ Delivered ∴ Free.

Be Sure to Call and Examine Before Buying Elsewhere.

804 THIRD AVENUE,

HUNTINGTON, W. VA.

Washington Jas. laborer, res alley b 3d and 4th av and 11th and 12th sts
Washington Mary, col'd, res alley b 3rd and 4th av and 11th and 12th sts
Washington Rose, col'd, res 825 5th av
Waters John, col'd, laborer, bds 819 2d av
Watkins David col'd, res 1676 8th av
Watkins Ed. engineer, rms 1032 7th av
Watkins Rosa, col'd, res 1676 8th av
Watkins William, fireman, res 1107 6th av
Watlington Robert, laborer, res cor 2d av and 3d st
Watts C. W. book-keeper, bds 1031 4th av
Watts E. L. hotel clerk, res 7th av hotel
Watts E. L. bar tender, bds 639 9th st
Waugh Carrie Mrs. dressmaker, res 1025 3d av
Waugh J. B. blacksmith, res 725 4th av
Waugh James P. laborer, res 1947 8th av
Waugh J. W. butcher, res 1025 3d av
Weaver Ed. timekeeper, res 3 Frame Row
Weaver Etta, dressmaker, res s s 3d av, West Huntington
Weaver J. H. contractor and builder, res s s 3d av, West Huntington
Weaver Lena, book-keeper, res s s 3d av, West Huntington
Weaver R. A. clerk, res s s 3d av, West Huntington
Webb Charles, boiler maker, res 1930 8th av
Webb Enoch, fireman, res 1903 8th av
Webb Ernest, painter, res 1930 8th av
Webb J. D. painter, res 1903 8th av
Webb Job, pattern maker, res 1032 6th av
Webb Nancy Mrs. cook, bds cor 8th st and 2d av
Webb W. N. B. tinner, res 1230 4th av
Weed Aaron, watchman, res 1948 8th av
Weekly Henry, laborer, bds 2 North Ensign
Welch Harry, painter, res 3d av, West Huntington
Welch Ida, gilder, res West Huntington
Welch John, carpenter, res 3 West Huntington
Welch William, painter, res 218 12th st
Wells Albert, hod carrier, res n alley b 11th and 12th sts
Wells Annie Mrs. seamstress, res 625 10th st
Wells A. G. carpenter, res 1845 4th av
Wells C. S. sawyer, res 1225 3d av
Wells Cecil, newsboy, res 1845 4th av
Wells Erna, teacher, res 625 10th st

Wells E. B. carpenter, res 1732 5th av
Wells Fannie, col'd, res 3d av b 11th and 12th sts
Wells Harry, engineer, res 625 10th st
Wells John, col'd, hod carrier, res alley b 11th and 12th sts North 3d av
Wells Leroy E. res 1225 3d av
Wells Minnie, servant, res 1542 2d av
Wells Melissa, dressmaker, res 1845 4th av
Wells Mrs. Nancy A. res 1732 5th av
Wells Ollie, artist, res 625 10th st
Wells Samuel W. laborer, res 1225 3d av
Wellman Addie, res 910 7th av
Wellman H. B. clerk, res 853 3d av
Wellman James, colored, barber, res cor 7th av and 16th st
Wellman Joseph, molder, res 1947 6th av
Wellman J. D. grocer, 841 7th av, res 910 7th av
Wellman M. F. barber, res cor 16th st and 7th av
Wellman William A. molder, res 1521 3d av
Werninger A. W. Catholic priest, res 1322 6th av
WERTZ HARRY, boiler maker, shop 1016 6th av alley, res 1016 6th av
West D. M. car inspector, res 1698 9th av
West Elihu, col'd, laborer, res 713 3d av
West Robert, col'd, res 1222 3d av
West W. E. trader, res 831 3d av
Wetherhalt Albert, laborer, res 1940 Buffington av
WETZEL L. F. M.D., physician and surgeon, res 1040 3d av
Wheaten Fanny, sales lady, res 1124 6th av
Wheaton Nelley, artist, res 1124 6th av
Wheaton W. C. picture frame maker, res 1124 6th av
Wheaton William, butcher, res 1124 6th av
Wheeler Amy J. res 812 3d av
Wheeler C. A. laborer, res 812 3d av
Wheeler Edward, engineer, res 828 7th av
Wheeler Henry, laborer, res 828 3d av
Wheeler H. A. molder, res 2431 1st av
Wheeler J. R. carpenter, res 3d av, West Huntington
Wheeler James, res 812 3d av
Wheeler Joseph, tinner, res 3d av, West Huntington
Wheeler Letitia, res 812 3d av
Wheeler Wirt, laborer, bds 3d av, W Huntington

Wheeler William S. teamster, res n s 2d av b 1st and 2d sts

White E. A. Mrs. res 914 7th av

White Ellen, col'd, cook, res alley b 11th and 12th sts n 3d av

White D. E. Mrs. res 1144 4th av

White Richard R. molder, res North 24th st

Whitehead Emma, res 1125 4th av

Whitehead Frank, carpenter, res 1125 4th av

Whitehead Frank, laborer, res 1419 4th av

Whitehead L. D. dressmaker, res 1125 4th av

Whitehead Nellie D. dressmaker, res 1125 4th av

Whitehead Robert, res 14th st near 11th av

Whitehead R. J. dressmaker, res 1125 4th av

Whitehead Rachel, dressmaker, res 1125 4th av

Whittaker J. C. teamster, 1118 3d av, res West Huntington

Whittaker Rowena, compositor, 308 10th st, bds West Huntington

Whitney E. E. Mrs. sales lady, res 1114 4th av

Whitney Frank, helper, bds 101 24th st

Whitney L. R. salesman, music dealer, res 1114 4th av

Wiatt J. R. shoe dealer, 938 3d av

Wiatt Susie, res 1342 3d

Wiatt Thomas A. lawyer, 916 3d av, res 1342 3d av

Wiatt W. O. timekeeper, res 1342 3d av

Wigner John, carpenter, res 1140 4th av

Wike Joseph, res 24 Buffington Row

Wilcox James, carpenter, bds 916 5th av

Wilcoxen Charles, tinner, 901 3d av, res 928 4th av

Wilcoxen Hattie, res 928 4th av

Wilcoxen H. Mrs. dressmaker, res 928 4th av

Wilcoxen Julia, teacher, res 928 4th av

Wilcoxen N. B. machine agent, 1042 3d av, res 928 4th av

Wiles Cora, bds 758 3d av

Wiley S. P. trader, 802 5th av, res same

Wilhelm Maggie, res 721 2d av

Wilhelm Otho, machinist, res 721 2d av

Wilhelm Wm. machinist, res 721 2d av

Wilhelm William, carpenter, res 721 2d av

Wilks Josie, seamstress, bds 1221 3d av alley

Wilkinson C. M. clerk, res 916 5th av

Wilkinson Edward V. res 916 5th av

Wilkinson W. E. blacksmith, res 916 4th av

Wilkinson W. E. boarding house, res 916 5th av
Willard Jane E. Mrs. res 1139 6th av
Wesley Willey, laborer, res 1723 4th av
Willis C. shoemaker, res 1902 4th av
Willis Laura, res 1902 4th av
Willis Mary, res 918 6th av
Willison Ancel, bds 1440 3d av
Willison George. res 1440 3d av
Willison Minnie, dressmaker, res 1440 3d av
Williams Asa L. retired merchant. res 1242 3d av
Williams Bettie, housework, res 827 4th av
Williams Charles B. artist, res n s 4th av. West Huntington
Williams Chester, teamster, res 1245 3d av
William Don, res 1005 4th av
Williams E. E. lawyer, 324 9th st, res 1728 5th av
Williams Mrs. Fannie, boarding house, res 1245 3d av
Williams Fannie L. saleslady, res 1245 3d av
Williams James, laborer, res 1119 4th av alley
Williams James H. engineer, res 1007 7th av
Williams J. F. distiller, res n s 4th av, West Huntington
Williams John, laborer, res 13 w Buffington av
Williams Lottie, res 737 2d st
Williams Mattie, dressmaker, res n s 4th av, West Huntington
Williams Minnie H. milliner, res 1245 3d av
Williams Maggie M. res n s 4th av, West Huntington
Williams Maggie, gilder, 927 2d av, res West Huntington
Williams Mollie, col'd, housework, res alley b 2d and 3d avs and 8th and 9th sts
Williams W. P. Mrs. boarding house, res 737 2d st
Williams Nannie L. Mrs. res n s 4th av, West Huntington
Williams Reese, car builder, res 1119 3d av
Williams Richard H. artist, res n s 4th av, West Huntington
Williams Rosa Mrs. res 1119 3d av
Williams B. W. col'd, blacksmith, res 523 20th st
Williams S. S. blacksmith, res 1746 4th av
Williams Sallie H. dressmaker, res n s 4th av, West Huntington
Williams W. H. foreman sawmill, res 1252 4th av
Williams W. C. res 1245 3d av
Williamson George, col'd, laborer, bds 1212 4th av alley
Williamson Robert H. conductor, res 720 6th av

HUNTINGTON [WIR] DIRECTORY.   133

Williamson W. M. res 523 10th st
Williamson William, res 1144 4th av
Willging Jane, col'd, res 815 2d av
Willging Thos. col'd, shop messenger, res 815 2d av
Wilson Mrs. Ammie, res 531 9th st
WILSON B. C. Clerk Circuit Court Cabell Co., Court
  House, res Marshall College
Wilson Charles R. res 531 9th st
Wilson Mrs. Emily, hotel, res 101 24th st
Wilson Miss G. B. res 531 9th st
Wilson G. I. salesman, bds 2d av cor 9th st
Wilson John, teamster, 1118 3d av, res 4th av, West Hunt-
  ington
Wilson Mrs. Jennie, housekeeper, res 3d av b 8th and 9th
  sts
Wilson John, laborer, bds 1916 Buffington av
Wilson John T. constable, 904 3d av res 531 9th st
Wilson Lou, res 101 24th st
Wilson Lottie Mrs. res 2211 3d av
Wilson Maria, res 419 11th st alley
Wilson S. col'd, restaurant, res 812 3d av
Wilson Theo. col'd, shooting gallery, res 810 3d av
Wilson W. B. grocer, 1001 10th st, res 529 12th st
Wilson W. L. book-keeper, res s e cor 10th st and 3d av
Winkler Lewis, stone cutter, res 1931 4th av
Wingfield C. W. express messenger, res 529 12th st
Winslow Fannie E. housekeeper, res 1005 4th av
Winslow Lucy A. housekeeper, res 1005 4th av
Winslow L. C. architect and sup't of buildings, res 1005
  4th av
Winslow Ruth M. housekeeper, res 1005 4th av
Winston Alex. col'd, laborer, res 215 12th st
Winston Mrs. Ella, col'd, res 215 12th st
Winston George, col'd, clerk, res 215 12th st
Winston Mrs. Sallie, col'd, housekeeper, res 215 12th st
Winstead Sally, col'd, housework, res 2d av b 8th and 9th
  sts
Winters Henry, barber, 937 3d av, res 3d av b 10th and
  11th sts
Winters J. W. barber, 308 9th st, bds cor 5th av and 9th st
Winters Lei, barber, 937 3d av, res 5th av b 8th and 9th
  sts
Wirthlin James, wharfmaster, res 1306 3d av

Wirthlin J. (W. & Marr), steamboat agent, foot 10th st, res n s 3d av b 13th and 14th st

Wirthlin & Marr, general steamboat agents, city wharf, foot 10th st

Wise John, machinist, bds 511 13th st

WITZGALL CHRIST, shoemaker, res 1953 3d av

WO DELL, Chinese Laundry, 748 3d av, res same

Wolf Alex. clerk, res 1038 4th av

Wolf Betty, res 1038 4th av

Wolf Benj. merchant, res 1038 4th av

Wolf Willie, compositor, res 825 3d av

Wollerton William. machinist, bds 2335 8th av

Womeldorff J. E. feed store and teaming, 1203 4th av, res 1215 3d av

Wood Charles, laborer. res 12 Buffington Row

Wood Carrie, res 925 6th av

Wood Edwin L. clerk, res 1021 6th av

Wood F. W. car builder, res 1707 Virginia av

Wood H. A. grocer, 933 6th av, res 1021 6th av 11th sts

Wood Hubert M. clerk, res 1021 6th av

Wood H. A. Mrs. clerk, res 1021 6th av

Wood J. E. contractor; res 1040 7th av

Wood Jennie, res 812 7th av

Wood Kate, student, bds 1021 5th av

Wood L. H. res 812 7th av

Wood Mamie. res 812 7th av

Wood Warren, pattern maker. res 925 6th av

Woodard M. A. Mrs. res 1018 6th av

Wooley Blanche, saleslady. res 940 5th av

Wooley Miss M. A. post office clerk, res 940 5th av

Wooley Mrs. M. M. res 940 5th av

Woodhull John, molder, res 1839 4th av

Woodman Robert, blacksmith, bds 1443 3d av

Woodrum John, carpenter. res 741 2d av

Woodrum Lewis, blacksmith, res 2325 8th av

Woods Charley, col'd, res cor 5th av and 4th st

Woods Emanuel, col'd, res cor 5th and 4th st

Woods Howard H. woodworker, res 1136 4th av

Woods James, machinist. res 930 7th av

Woods M. E. core maker. res 1305 14th st

Woods Manuel, col'd, servant 1322 3d av

Woods Nettie. cook, res 1955 3d av

Woods Peter, col'd, carpenter, res cor 5th av and 4th st

Woods Richard, foreman, res 1136 4th av
Woods Wm. E. machinist, res 1134 4th av
Woodrum Cora, res 2325 8th av
Woodson Robert A. col'd, laborer, res 813 8th st
Wooten J. P. painter, res 223 3d av
Wooten L. carpenter, res 2541 1st av
Wooten Miss L. C. dressmaker, res 2541 1st av
Wooten M. V. B. contractor, res 2541 1st av
Woodworth A. H. clerk, res 1226 3d av
Woodworth Alvah, res 1226 3d av
Worden A. J. laborer, res 7 Buffington Row
Worden Mary M. res 7 Buffington Row
Worden V. V. res 7 Buffington Row
Worden W. F. laborer, res 7 Buffington Row
Workman Clara, housework, 1314 3d av
Workman Randolph, laborer, res 817 av alley
Worley Clara E. dressmaker, res 1918 8th av
Worley John J. G. carpenter, res 1918 8th av
Wray Miss Rainy, res 814 3d av
Wray Wilson, drayman, res 814 3d av
Wright Annie, res 925 3d av
Wright D. R. laborer, res 1838 5th av
Wright Elizabeth, res 835½ 2d av
Wright Fred, conductor, res 1107 6th av
Wright Fred, core maker, res 1954 7th av
Wright George, laborer, res 1838 5th av
Wright H. L. paving contractor, res 647 3d av
Wright Ira, res 1838 5th av
Wright J. A. carpenter, res 747 4th av
Wright J. J. molder, res 2346 1st av
Wright Lottie, res 647 3rd av
Wright Lee, machinist, res 1954 7th av
Wright Retta, res 1954 7th av
Wright Samuel, cooper, 847 res 2d av
Wright Samuel U. artist, 908 4th av, res 3d av alley
Wright T. L. machinist, res 419 8th st
Wright Wm. bds 8 Frame Row
Wright Wm. col'd, res 7th av hotel
Wyatt A. E. Miss, res 940 7th av
Wyatt Belle Mrs. res 940 7th av
Wyatt Hattie, res 1340 4th av
Wyatt J. E. Miss, res 940 7th av
Wyatt J. M. express agent, 1038 3d av, res 1340 4th av
Wyatt Mattie, res 1340 4th av